TURN OF THE
MOON

NEW YORK TIMES AND *USA TODAY* BESTSELLING AUTHOR
L.P. DOVER

All rights reserved. No part of this book may be reproduced or transmitted in any form by any means, electronic or mechanical, including photocopying, recording, or by any information storage and retrieval system, without written consent from the author.

L.P. Dover
Copyright © by L.P. Dover
Edited by: Victoria Schmitz | Crimson Tide Editorial
Cover designed by: RBA Designs

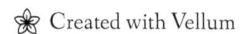

Created with Vellum

INTRODUCTION

This is my first dabble in paranormal and I have to say I fell in love with it. My wolves remind me of my MMA fighters (Gloves Off series) just with the ability to shift. I'm sure that'll make some of you happy. I love me some alpha males. Anyway, I just want to say thank you for giving my new adventure a chance. It was fun being able to write about hot, sexy shifters for a change.

ONE

BAILEY

"I'm sorry but there's no other way, Bailey. We gave you a whole extra year to come to terms with this," my father grumbled.

I quickened my pace toward the meadow, my jaw aching from clenching too hard. "I was hoping you'd come to your senses, but obviously not. I can't believe you did this to me! I'm not going to agree to this . . . I won't."

"You have no choice, Bailey. We did what we thought would keep you safe. You're of age now, and mating with Kade will keep you safe and pass on our bloodline."

Actually, I *did* have a choice. My father was alpha of our pack, but my loyalties remained my own. I didn't feel the pull that everyone else did when it came to following orders. While they had to follow them; I didn't. Growing up, I had often wondered if there was something wrong with me. But as I got older, it all began to make sense. I had a gift—I was a rare female alpha—and it needed to stay hidden.

"Keep me *safe*? You've got to be kidding me. I've kept myself safe my entire life. Maybe I should've left when I had the chance." They both tensed and hung back while I took the lead.

They were angry, yet it was almost as if they were scared of fighting against me, afraid I would leave and never return. I wanted to do what was best for our pack, I really did. But mating with Kade wasn't the answer. I was basically being given away like a mail-order bride.

There was a time when I lived for the pack, when I would do anything to save my people. The white wolves were slowly reducing in number, and now everyone was desperate, struggling to make ends meet before we were wiped into extinction. I was twenty-four years old, and a daughter of the Northern pack alpha. It was my duty to continue my lineage. The only problem was, there were no other unmated alphas around other than my best friend, Sebastian, and the supreme douche, Kade Whitemore.

There was no way in hell I was going to alliance myself with that rat bastard. He was alpha of the Yukon pack, violent, and an overbearing ass who'd rather see me on my back with my legs spread open than being his equal. I'd rather die than be forced to be his mate for all eternity. Why couldn't I mate with Sebastian? Thinking of fucking him gave me the willies, but anything was better than Kade.

Anger racked my body and I sat there, seething . . . until I felt him. He was coming for me; I could sense him drawing near. The closer we got to the meadow, the more I could smell Kade and his excitement—his lust. Hopefully, he could smell the rage and disgust coming from me.

Wolves mated for life; it was a sacred union. It wasn't like a human marriage where you could end it by signing a piece of paper. Our unions weren't something you did lightly. It was also not a decision I was going to let my parents make for me. The only way to escape would be to kill him, and the last thing I wanted to do was start a war between packs. There had to be another way.

Up ahead, in wolf form, Kade kept his stare dialed in on me. He was large—like all alpha males tended to be—but I wasn't impressed. He could smell my indifference and in return growled low, challenging me. I glared straight at him, not backing down, nor lowering my head. No one would ever make me submit.

Shifters needed the magic of the moon to change into their wolf form, but the strongest of our kind could transform at any time of the day. Most of the wolves in our pack had that advantage, except on the nights of the new moon. Only alphas had the ability to change on those nights. Tonight, there was no moon, so being the arrogant jackass he was, Kade decided to show up as his wolf. *Figures.*

Everyone backed away except me and my father. Kade sidled up to us and brushed his body against mine, marking me. Next, he pushed his nose between my legs and sniffed. Anger consumed me and I was close to shifting, but held back. "You do that shit again and I'll have me a nice, white fur coat for the winter."

His lips pulled back in a wolfish grin before he transformed into his naked, human self. "I was only getting a taste of what's mine."

Most white wolves had similar traits—light colored hair and blue eyes, with the occasional exception of green. My parents both had the bright blonde hair and had passed it down to me, along with their crystal blue eyes and immaculate strength. However, their strength wasn't with them today which made me wary. My father didn't even attempt to defend my honor.

Raking my gaze over Kade, he had platinum blond hair, striking blue eyes, and a body that even I hadn't seen on the men in my pack. He was much larger, in more ways than one, and one of the youngest alphas in the country, most likely in his late twenties by the looks of him. Fortunately, when his gaze found mine, I didn't see my future mate in those eyes.

Crossing my arms at my chest, I stood stock-still, waiting on my father to get done talking to him. I only wished he'd take heed of my loathing and leave. I wasn't going to go with him. Everyone else got the choice of who they mated with and I'll be damned if I didn't get the same luxury.

Back and forth the men conversed heatedly, the tension filling the cool night air. The moment my father's blue eyes met mine, I knew something was wrong. *Please, don't let it be so.* He clutched my face in his hands and kissed me on the head. "Say goodbye to the pack. By sunrise, you'll be on your way with Kade to your new home."

"What?" I shouted, pulling away. "You're supposed to be our alpha! Are you really so spineless?"

Our pack sucked in a collective breath at my daring words. Kade smirked and I made sure he could feel every ounce of my hatred. I pushed my power so hard at him, he stumbled back.

My dad was working hard on biting his tongue. "To ensure the survival of our packs, and to keep you safe, there's no other way. We have to honor our promise."

"Fuck your promise, and fuck you," I hissed. "It was yours, not mine."

"It was the packs, Bailey. There's no way around it."

There's a way around everything. My power roiled but I couldn't unleash it . . . yet. It wasn't the right time. Taking a deep breath, I closed my eyes and huffed. "I'd like to speak to my intended for a moment, alone. I'll say my goodbyes to everyone once we're done."

My father nodded in agreement and walked away, looking back at me once before turning his back. My pack followed close behind him, along with my mother who had tears streaming down her cheeks. The Yukon pack, however . . .

"Your people need to go," I demanded.

Glancing over his shoulder, Kade nodded to his second in command and they disappeared through the trees.

When they were out of earshot, I pursed my lips and spat, "Out of every single pack in the world, you came to this one to claim me. Surely you could find someone who'd be glad to take you."

"True, but I wanted *you*."

"What makes you think I'm going to leave with you tomorrow?"

Kade laughed and sauntered over, leaning close so he could smell me; I stood my ground and didn't waver, even when he brushed up against me. I could rip his heart out in the blink of an eye. He moaned and grew hard between his legs. "You're mine, Bailey," he growled, circling around behind me. "You were promised to me, and I'm not leaving without you."

"You don't even know me."

Pushing his cock against my ass, he reached around and placed his large hands on my thighs, holding me to him. Wolves were physical creatures and we loved touch, but I didn't want him touching me.

"So help me God, if you don't back up, I'm going to rip out your goddamned throat."

Instead of letting me go, he held me tighter and chuckled in my ear, rubbing his scent all over my body. His hands gripped my breasts, and then one slid down into my pants so he could cup me with his palm. "I'd like to see you try, sweetheart. I love a good fight. The more you resist, the harder I'm going to fuck you."

His pheromones were extremely high, choking me, and with that I could smell his need to mate, to claim me. I needed to do something fast without unleashing my power. I struggled in his hold, but the more I moved against him, the wilder his scent grew. He wanted the fight, and I couldn't give him what he wanted.

Taking a deep breath, I swallowed back the bile and leaned into his touch, putting one of my hands over the one he had down my pants. I had to make him believe I didn't want to fight. All I needed was a little bit of time.

Rubbing my ass against his cock, I took hold of his fingers and pushed one inside me, and then another. I gasped as his growl deepened and he bit down hard on my neck, drawing blood. *Fucking bastard.* Biting your mate was an intimate act only to be done when you're actually mated.

"Now everyone will know you're mine," he whispered gruffly in my ear. "I'm going to fuck you until you scream. I've waited long enough to get you, and now that I have you, there's no escape."

"I tell you what," I rasped, slowly trying to pull away, "why don't I go tell my family goodbye, and then you can do whatever you want with me."

Gripping my arms, he turned me around and ripped my shirt off my body, making me gasp. He lowered his mouth to one of my nipples and sucked hard while pushing his fingers back inside of me. "Actually, I have a better idea. How about you put that mouth of yours around my cock and then you can say goodbye. You need to start acting like my mate and do as I say."

Gripping me around the waist, he forced my pants down and knocked me backward onto the ground. The breath whooshed out of my lungs and I choked, struggling to suck in a breath as he put his weight on top of me. "Don't worry, sweetheart, you'll enjoy it."

Immediately, I could feel my fangs lengthen behind my lips and my body temperature rise. I was so close to shifting. As alpha, my fangs were longer, sharper. I could be in human form and still rip someone to shreds with my teeth.

I refused to be a victim for the sake of my pack.

"Kade," I moaned, opening my legs for him. "Take me now." All I needed was a clear shot to his neck. I had been with human men before, but never another wolf. I'd heard it was the best sex ever, and I planned on experiencing it one day . . . but not yet.

Chuckling, Kade lifted his head and I hid my fangs behind my closed lips. "Begging me already? I'm disappointed, little wolf. I thought you would put up more of a fight."

When he lowered his mouth to my breasts, I could feel the tip of his cock pushing on my opening. The tension in his body elevated and I knew I needed to act fast. Before he could thrust inside, I opened my mouth wide and locked them on the inside of his neck. In one quick move, I ripped out as much flesh as I could. His blood ran warm down my throat, making me gag. I spit it out, along with a giant mound of flesh from his body.

Falling over to the side, he grabbed his throat and gurgled, choking on his own blood. I refused to be a slave to him when I was more powerful. Holding the wound on his neck, he growled as his eyes started to change into that of his wolf. He tried to shift, but it wasn't working.

As I jumped to my feet, Kade grabbed a hold of my ankle and I fell to the ground.

"You're going . . . to pay . . . bitch."

I needed to get away before the packs could hear our struggle. Luckily, I wriggled out of his hold and kicked his hand away. Knowing he would be dead in a matter of minutes, I summoned my magic and let the force shimmer around my body. Kade's eyes went wide in disbelief. Letting the magic overtake me, I shifted into my wolf form and took off. I never once looked back. I didn't want to leave everyone behind, but they left me no choice.

I would never see my family again.

TWO

BAILEY

For days, I traveled through the wilderness, keeping to the forests as I crossed the border from Canada to the United States. I had never been that far south, and I didn't know where to go or what to do, considering I had no clothes or money. I would rather be a lone wolf than spend the rest of my eternity with an abusive jackass. I'd never seen any of our male wolves treat their mates like that, and I sure as hell wasn't going to let anyone be that way to me.

Once I made it to the mountains in Wyoming, I was beyond exhausted. Thankfully, Kade's scent had worn off to where I couldn't smell him anymore. My paws hurt, I was filthy, and I was so hungry I could eat a whole deer—if I wasn't too tired to hunt one. I could survive as a wolf for as long as I needed to, but I missed the amenities of everyday life. A nice, hot shower would've felt great.

It was then a smell of a crisp, clean lake floated past my face. It was just up ahead. Making my way there, I noticed it was mostly frozen and nestled in a small valley between snow-capped mountains. Luckily, there were still parts of it that weren't frozen, which reflected the moon's light. The water was way below freezing, but being an Arctic wolf I could withstand those temperatures with no problems at all.

Looking around, I knew there was nothing close by other than a couple of smaller animals and a bear that was about a mile away. I wanted to make sure it was safe before shifting. Once Kade's pack started looking for me, I'd be a hunted wolf. I didn't want to run for the rest of my life, but I had no choice.

Stepping into the water, I walked down the rocky slope and shifted. Holding my breath, I completely submerged myself, letting the cool, fresh water cleanse me. I ran my hands over my body and through my hair to make sure every place Kade touched had been washed thoroughly. He'd made me feel dirty from the inside out.

After a few extra seconds submerged under the water, I lifted my head and took in a deep, ragged breath. I always wanted freedom, but running for the rest of my life wasn't what I considered being free. Slowly, I started out of the lake but came to a halt.

I wasn't alone anymore.

The wind had blown the scent of a nearby wolf in my direction and it wasn't just any type of wolf. It was an Arctic, just like me. He wasn't one of Kade's pack or mine, but it was still dangerous being out in the woods alone without my pack's support.

Quickly rushing out of the water, I crouched behind a set of bushes. I breathed in again, hoping I was just being paranoid. But there was definitely another wolf around and it was an unmated alpha male. He was about half a mile away and moving closer by the second. Closing my eyes, I transformed into my wolf and darted out of the bushes and away from the lake. From the vibrations on the ground, he faltered for a second and stopped before picking up his pace. I was tired and weak, hoping like hell I could outrun him.

The answer came swiftly enough when I heard his growls behind me, only a few feet away. *Don't look back*, I chanted over and over in my mind. My muscles burned and started to shake, but I had to keep going. After only another couple of minutes of racing through the forest, I came to a complete halt when the mysterious white wolf lunged and landed on my back. My body gave out and my legs buckled underneath.

When I recovered from the fall, I was pinned to the ground, the other wolf staring curiously at me with his glowing emerald eyes. There was no hostility or any indication he wanted to hurt me, yet when I smelled other wolves approaching, all I could think about was fleeing. Slipping out from under his hold, I bolted through the trees but didn't get very far.

The last thing I saw before everything went black were those emerald green eyes staring down at me. Except this time they weren't coming from a wolf, they were from the most handsome face I'd ever seen.

They were almost familiar . . .

THREE

RYKER

"Is that really her? What the hell is she doing all the way down here?" Cedric asked.

Bailey had turned back into her human self almost immediately after subduing her. She was too weak to keep hold of her magic, which was why she was limp in my arms as I carried her through the woods to the ranch. The rest of the pack followed closely behind in wolf form. "I don't know. The last I checked she was still in her territory."

"What are you going to do with her?" he asked.

"Hell if I know. She looks at me like she has no fucking clue who I am. I don't get it."

"Are you going to tell her?"

"When she wakes up."

"Why do you not sound happy about that? All the guys in the pack would give their left nut to find their mate."

I snorted. "You don't know Bailey. She's an alpha female. Need I say more?"

"Have the visions started yet? You drew blood when you bit her."

And I could still taste her on my lips. Even if I didn't

know she was my mate, her blood would've been answer enough. "No, they haven't, but I can feel the connection. Her mind is starting to open up."

"What's going on in there?" he asked, excitement in his voice.

"Not that I would actually tell you, but right now it's nothing but quick flashes. I can't tell what they are."

"Man, I bet she's going to be pissed when she wakes up."

"I have no doubt." I was going to have my hands full. Even when I met her years ago, she was a spitfire.

Cedric slapped me on the shoulder and laughed. "Better you than me, bro. I doubt she'll put up a fight for long though."

"I wouldn't bet on it," I grumbled. We finally reached the ranch and I made sure the pack kept their distance.

"Do you want me to get the council together? They'll want to know what's going on." The council was simply the alphas of each pack in the surrounding areas—my allies.

I looked down at Bailey. "Send word. It shouldn't take long for them to arrive. They'll want to know if trouble's coming. I have no doubt Bailey's pack will come looking for her."

"And what if they attack?"

Stopping at the door, I sighed. If they came looking for her, they'd fight to get her back. "I'll kill them."

I carried Bailey inside and went straight to my bedroom to lay her down. Now that I'd drank her blood, I could get in her head. I wanted to know what made her run from her pack, but all that was showing in her mind were flashes of me and the woods. It was strange seeing myself through her eyes.

Tucking her platinum blonde hair behind her ear, I leaned down close, breathing her in. "Bailey, wake up."

She stirred with my touch but her eyes stayed closed. One of the first things about the bond was that we could see visions of our future. I thought it would've happened as soon as I'd tasted her blood, but it hadn't yet.

A few hours later, I could hear a couple of the other alphas approaching. Sliding off the bed, I grabbed a T-shirt and jeans out of my closet and threw them on before making my way out to the living room. Thankfully, with the bond, I didn't have to worry about Bailey trying to escape.

There were five alphas, including myself, but only two had shown up, Ian and Tate. The others had a longer distance to travel. Cedric nodded and disappeared out the door to stand guard.

"Thanks for coming on such short notice," I greeted as they entered.

The Northwestern pack alpha, Ian Randale, came forward and shook my hand. He was my age and an unmated gray wolf who was tall with light brown hair and green eyes. In fact, all of the alphas in the council were unmated. Ian, however, was one of the youngest alphas to ever receive the title. He defeated the original alpha at only fifteen years old, through combat no less. The alpha before him had been a fucking Machiavellian douchebag. We were all ready to see him go.

"No worries." He bent his head in greeting. "I'm here to help."

"Me as well," the other alpha agreed, shaking my hand. His name was Tate Grayson, leader of the Great Plains pack. He had dark brown hair and blue eyes; the exact imitation of his father who had stepped down as alpha and made him their pack's leader.

My story was different; I was chosen by the entire pack.

"Thank you. And you know I wouldn't have called if it wasn't important."

Ian's brows furrowed. "What's going on?"

I glanced at them both. "I found my mate."

Their eyes went wide. "But no one has found their true mate in years," Tate remarked.

"Until now. I've known who mine was for years. I could just never get to her because of her pack. Now she's here."

"I'm happy for you . . . but what does that have to do with us?" Ian asked.

I blew out a heavy sigh. "I'm pretty sure her pack is going to start looking for her. There could be other wolves coming into your territories asking about her. I want you to be ready."

His muscles tensed. "Are we talking a simple formality, or war?"

"There won't be a war unless they come here demanding her. If they do, I can handle them on my own. I just want you both to be prepared." They both nodded and it was a huge relief.

Out of nowhere, visions from Bailey's mind blasted into my head. They were vivid and not the simple flashes from before. Not only were they full-on dreams, but in them I was claiming her. I could hear her screams and feel her nails down my back as I plunged in deep. It was as if I was actually there experiencing it. Holy fuck, I was about to explode.

"You okay, brother?" Tate asked, zapping me out of my thoughts.

No, I wasn't okay. I had a raging hard on. Clearing my throat, I put my hands in my pockets to cover the bulge. "I'm fine. The visions seem to be starting up."

They both chuckled, knowing very well what I was referring to. Ian spoke first, "I know what that means. My grandfather told me stories. He said he couldn't leave the house without jacking off at least twice during the bonding phase. But you know, that was when they were made to wait until the full moon to bond."

"I doubt she'll want anything to do with me at the moment. I only got a taste of her blood during a fight. She wasn't exactly willing."

Smirking, Tate shook his head. "Something tells me you wanted to bite her though. Am I right?"

As much as I wanted to deny it, I couldn't. She bore my mark and every male who got near her would know she was mine, mated or not. "What can I say?"

Ian patted me on the shoulder. "Good luck with your hand tonight."

"Thanks," I grumbled.

He started for the door with Tate behind him. "Oh, and if her pack does come for her, I'll stand behind you."

I gave my appreciation and then glanced at Tate who nodded.

"My pack will too. I never thought I'd see the day when the magic returned to our people. Maybe I'll even get lucky one day."

Once they were out the door, I headed back upstairs and it took every ounce of strength I had not to get on the bed with Bailey. "Fuck me," I groaned, salivating over her smooth, naked skin. All I wanted to do was spread her wide and fuck her senseless. I'd wanted to do that every day since I saw her in college. It enraged me to see her around human men. I didn't like them touching her or breathing around her, but there was nothing I could do at the time.

The blankets over Bailey's body slid all the way down to

her waist when she moved. Moaning, she arched her back off the bed, her nipples inviting me to taste them. In her mind, I had my mouth wrapped around them, sucking hard while I pushed inside her. It was like a fucking porno movie in my mind. There was only one thing I could do.

Unzipping my jeans, I pulled my cock out and wrapped my hand around it. It was going to be one hell of a night.

FOUR

BAILEY

"I take it you don't want to go back with me." Sebastian's eyebrows raise up as he puts my bags in the trunk and slams it shut.

I look straight into my best friend's bright blue eyes and they spark with power. "Would you want to go back to a cage?" I had enjoyed my freedom at college, but I know as soon as I step back into the pack, my life will not be my own anymore.

Sighing, he opens the car door. "You might think you're alone in this, but you're not. Things will change, B. I just need you to give it a little more time."

I snort. "Time? I don't even know what the hell you're talking about. I am alone, Sebastian. The only people I have are you and my parents. Everyone else stays away from me."

"I'm sure your parents missed you."

"And you didn't?"

Chuckling, he runs a hand through his bright blond hair. "I missed your smart-ass mouth. It was boring while you were away. You always had a way of keeping me entertained."

I lean against the car and smile. "I'm surprised my father hasn't asked you to be my mate."

His grin disappears as he looks away. "I think Darius has other plans."

"Like what?" As soon as I ask, my skin tingles and burns. A mysterious wolf is near. His power calls to mine and I want to succumb, but I will not go down that easily.

Sebastian narrows his eyes, studying me, and then goes into full alert. "Bailey, get in the car." His eyes focus on something across the street and I know who it is without even looking. He's a wolf and an alpha. For the past five years, I had sensed him near, but he never once approached. Not until now. "Get in the fucking car, Bailey," Sebastian growls again.

I don't want to get in the car. Instead, I turn around and get my first glimpse of the mysterious wolf. He's standing beside a black Jeep with his arms crossed angrily at his chest. His light brown hair is hidden underneath a navy baseball cap, and he's dressed in a white T-shirt and ripped jeans. His bright green eyes meet mine and my wolf stirs deep inside, calling to him. The only word floating through my mind is something I am not expecting.

Mine.

Our eyes meet, but the connection breaks when Sebastian forces me into the car. "What the fuck is wrong with you?" He slams the door and gets in, squealing the tires as he races us down the street and away from the green-eyed wolf. I look back through the window and he is gone.

My world shimmers and I am sucked into another place and time.

Hands hold me down, but it's not out of aggression, it's passion fueled. I moan as the green eyed wolf pushes himself into me, claiming me. I love the way his skin feels against mine and the way we move together. I've never felt so close to anyone before. It's almost as if we're connected somehow.

"Bailey, wake up," a voice called. It was the voice in my dreams, the voice of the wolf.

When I finally woke up, I wasn't in the woods . . . and I definitely wasn't alone. *His* scent surrounded me, not only in the air, but on my body. *What the hell?* Clenching my teeth, I growled and tried to roll off the bed, with no such luck. Apprehended, with an arm across my stomach, I felt him straddle my waist, chuckling as he pinned my arms above my head.

"Let me go," I demanded, glaring up into his glowing gaze. His touch made my body tingle, almost like an electrical current passing from his body to mine. It was strange, yet I welcomed it, even though my mind was telling me to knee him in the junk.

"Good morning to you too, Sleeping Beauty. I trust you're well rested?" he asked, smiling wide. I half expected him to look at my body, but he kept his focus on my eyes. Point for him.

My cheeks burned. "I slept fine. But if you don't get off of me, I'm going to make sure you choke on your balls. Your choice."

He smirked and rolled off. There was a T-shirt on the edge of the bed he snatched up and slipped on. He wasn't mated, because if he was I would smell another female on him. There was nothing other than the woods, the unique scent of our Arctic bloodline, and something else. I just couldn't place what that other smell was.

"Calm down, Bailey. You know very damn well I'm not going to hurt you."

I snatched the blanket off the bed and wrapped it around me, huffing. "You're right, you're not." He laughed and it only pissed me off more. "How do you know my name?"

Staring at me with those hypnotic eyes, he ran a hand through his tousled, light blond hair. "I've known you for a long time now."

"You mean stalked," I clarified. I had to admit, he was a good looking stalker. All I could think of was wrapping my legs around his body and gripping that hair of his while he spread me wide. I could see it clearly in my mind from my dream. It felt so real, as if it actually happened.

He chuckled darkly and bit his lip. "Oh, it will happen, angel. What you saw and did in your dream was our future. It wasn't easy sleeping beside you when I couldn't touch you."

Eyes wide, I jumped out of the bed and backed against the wall, clutching the blanket tight. "How the hell did you know what I was thinking?" Surely, I didn't say it out loud. I was about to go into full panic mode when a calm swept through my body like warm lavender. I didn't feel like myself. "What's going on?" I whispered.

Cautiously, he edged closer. "Bailey, it's okay. My name's Ryker. I want to help you, not hurt you. Through our bond I can calm you down, but I can't do it forever. Right now, I need you to listen to me. There's so much I need to tell you."

"Through our bond? What are you talking about?"

Holding out his hand, he beckoned me closer. "Here, take my hand and tell me what you feel."

I stared at his hand before he snatched mine instead. Immediately, my body lit up like fire, coursing through every vein. I could feel each emotion inside of him like they were my own. There was passion, happiness, concern, and even . . . love. How could that be? The longer I touched him, the more I wanted—the more I craved. I didn't want to let go.

"Why do I feel like this when I don't even know you?" I asked.

Ryker pulled me close, and all I wanted was for him to put his arms around me, to touch me with those strong hands of his. "You do know me, Bailey. It was a long time ago, but I knew I would never forget your face as long as I lived."

Eyes wide, I gasped. "When? Where? I don't remember you other than seeing you in my dreams a little bit ago. Well, that, and your eyes seem familiar. Why do they seem familiar?" I muttered the last question to myself.

Tucking a strand of my hair behind my ear, he smiled and caressed my cheek. "I was there the day that other wolf picked you up from college. I was pissed when I saw you leave with him. The day I was able to come for you, was the day I lost you."

"So the dream actually happened? Why don't I remember you from that day? And how could you even sense me? I was under a shielding spell. No other wolves should've been able to find me."

"Magic doesn't work against a mate, angel. Don't get me wrong, whatever voodoo shit you had surrounding you made it difficult, but I was still able to find you. I had to tread carefully when you went back to Canada, however."

"Oh my God, how is this even possible? I've never heard of mates being able to do that." I'd never actually heard anything about what happened when wolves mated. I felt so lost. Letting go of his hand, I stepped back. "Whatever you're doing to my emotions, stop."

The warmth went away and I was back to feeling in control. I had to get out of there. I thought Ryker would try to stop me, but he didn't as I stalked past him and down the stairs. There was nowhere to go but out. The magic grew inside me and as soon as I opened the door, I was ready to shift. Unfortunately, there were six wolves standing guard.

"You have got to be kidding me."

"I MUST REALLY BE dangerous to need six babysitters," I grumbled. What had me confused was the mish mash of wolves standing before me. They weren't all Arctic's like myself and Ryker, but different grays, and even a red one. I'd never known an alpha to be over a pack with different breeds.

I'd been outside for two hours, sitting on the front porch with only a blanket wrapped around my body. The ranch had a picturesque view of the Grand Teton Mountains, surrounded by nothing but land and trees. It was the perfect place for a wolf. I had heard about the area and read stories about its beauty, but I never thought I'd actually see it. There was snow all over the peaks and I longed to feel it under my paws.

Unfortunately, there was no way I could do that with glowing eyes staring back at me from every corner. I was beginning to think I was back in the confinements of my own pack. They watched over me the exact same way, afraid I'd run away if I ever got the chance. I left one prison for another.

As if my wishes were heard, the wolves scattered. But then the sound of a car traveling over a gravel driveway could be heard. I started to get up and Ryker appeared in the doorway, dressed in a park ranger uniform. He regarded me warily before nodding toward the car.

"Tyla's here to keep you company."

"You mean 'make sure I don't run away.'"

Sighing, he strapped the gun into his belt and faced me. By the look in his eyes, I felt terrible for snapping at him. "You're not a prisoner here, Bailey. I want you to feel free to go and do as you please. Tyla's here to show you around and be your friend. If running away is what you want, then go. I'm not going to force anything on you."

I studied him, narrowing my gaze. "Do you mean that?"

He gently took my hand, rubbing his thumb over my knuckles. My skin tingled like it always did when he touched me. I didn't want him to let go, but he did. "I do."

"What's up, guys?" Tyla shouted with a wide grin on her face. She had shoulder length, curly blonde hair and gray eyes, not an Arctic wolf but a gray. She seemed friendly enough.

"That's why I thought she'd be a good match for you," Ryker murmured.

"Okay, listening in on my thoughts is getting kind of weird."

"Don't worry, I don't listen to everything you say. But I do know you're hungry. Anyone from a mile away could hear your stomach growling. Tyla's going to take you to get something to eat."

I looked down at the blanket. "In what? I don't have any clothes."

Tyla reached into the backseat of her silver sports car and held it up. "Now you do, sunshine. Let's get you cleaned up. I'm starved." She ran up the steps and patted Ryker on the shoulder. "She'll be fine, boss. We girls are going to have some fun."

He shook his head, a small smile splaying across his lips. "Not *too* much." She winked and sauntered through the door, bag in hand. Chuckling, he turned back to me, smile disappearing. I liked his smile. "I'll be back tonight. I'm hoping you'll be here when I return. There's a lot you still don't know."

I watched him walk to his truck and drive away, glancing back at me once before disappearing down the road. "You aren't seriously thinking of leaving are you?" Tyla asked, crossing her arms over her chest.

Turning to her, I glared straight into her eyes. "What if I was? You gonna stop me?" I challenged.

She lowered her eyes and her head. "No. I'm no match for your power. But I do think you need to give Ryker and our pack a chance."

I stepped past her into the house and sighed. "You wouldn't feel that way if you knew what I'd done."

After shutting the door, she stood in front of me, handing me the bag of clothes. "The past doesn't matter. You're Ryker's mate and a true born alpha. I've never met another wolf like you before. It's nice to have a female around who could kick some serious ass."

She made me laugh and it felt good. "I'm sure you could too. You don't take me as the type to put up with much bullshit."

"I don't, especially when I'm starving. Now, run upstairs and get dressed. I'm taking you to one of my favorite restaurants." I stood there, staring at her like she'd lost her mind. "Why do you look like that?" she asked.

I shrugged. "I don't know. The way you all do things is so much different than what I'm accustomed to. My parents let me go away to college and I loved the freedom, but when I was back with the pack, I was never able to leave the compound. I guess I just figured it'd be like that here."

"Hell no," she exclaimed, bursting out in laughter. "We have our own homes, jobs, everything. Don't get me wrong, we hunt and do a lot of stuff together, but we live like normal human beings. Ryker would never keep you on a leash."

It was nice to hear that, but I knew I couldn't stay long. The Yukon Pack would kill them all to get to me. Plastering on a fake smile, I started for the stairs. "Thank you for the clothes. I'll be right down." I took a quick shower and put on some jeans and a pink blouse from the bag, along with the pair of boots. It felt good to take a shower. It'd been over a week since my last.

Tyla waited by the door when I got downstairs. "Ready to experience true freedom?"

"You have no idea." We hopped in her car and she sped us out of the driveway. I was mesmerized by the mountains, by the snow; it was breathtaking. "It's so beautiful here," I said.

"Yes, it is. I'm assuming you didn't see much of this where you came from?"

I shook my head, wishing like hell I could forget everything that happened. "No, and I definitely don't want to talk about it."

"Okay, we won't talk about it then. How about when you went away to school? What did you major in?"

I glanced out the window and smiled. "Teaching."

"What subject?"

"Chemistry," I answered, turning to face her. "I loved working with high school kids."

She pulled into a steak house parking lot and turned off the car. My stomach growled even louder than before. "You could get a job at one of the local high schools! The school year is basically over, but I'm sure you could find one for next fall."

We got out of the car and headed for the door. "Are you serious?" Excitement fluttered in my belly.

"Yeah, why wouldn't I be? If getting a job makes you happy, Ryker will be all for it. Not to mention, you could keep an eye on some of our rowdy teenagers. They'd behave knowing one of our alphas was watching over them."

The thought was so tempting, I actually considered it. But I couldn't do anything until I knew I was safe from the Yukon pack. "I'll have to think on it. Again, I don't know if I'm staying."

Inside, the hostess sat us at a table and got our drinks. I was so hungry, I ordered two appetizers, an entrée, and dessert. One good thing about being a wolf was, I didn't have to worry about calorie consumption. Eating every single bite, I garnered curious glares from our waitress every time she walked by. I guess I'd be like that too if I saw someone scarfing down a meal for two.

Sitting back in my chair, I focused on Tyla. "So what exactly do you do around here? Do you work?"

She nodded. "At a ranch down the road from Ryker's." Her phone rang, so she grabbed it out of her back pocket and looked at it. "Speak of the devil. It's Blake, the guy I work for." They talked for a few minutes, but I chose not to listen into their conversation. Tyla was watching me to see if I was.

After the call, she paid for our food and then we headed on our way.

"What exactly do you do on the ranch?"

"You're about to find out. Blake needs help with a horse he just bought."

"Is he human?"

"Yep. He moved out here about eight months ago, a city boy from Charlotte, North Carolina. Anyway, he inherited the ranch from his grandfather which is who I originally worked for. Blake had no clue how to manage it when he came. So I helped him, along with most of the pack. He's good friends with Ryker."

"Does he know what we are?"

She shook her head. "Ryker doesn't want him to know. I wanted to change him, but my request was denied. My parents say to give the old magic a chance."

"Old magic?"

We drove past the entrance to Ryker's ranch until we came to another one with a sign that read *Three Bar Ranch* at the top. She turned down the gravel path and drove slow. "You really don't know what old magic is?" When I shook my head, she looked nonplussed. "I'm sorry, that's just . . . so strange. I thought it was basic knowledge for every wolf. What the hell did your parents teach you?"

I clenched my teeth. "Obviously, not a lot. They never even told me about true mates."

"I see that. I'm sure Ryker will tell you all about it. Anyway, the old magic is the way things used to be in the past. My parents are true mates, the way you and Ryker are . . . or will be, eventually. Many of us wait our whole lives to find that one person. It used to not be like that. Before, you could find your mate easily."

"What if you don't?"

She parked the car and looked out the window. "Then we either, find someone else and never be truly happy, or we turn someone. The latter is frowned upon, but some have done it. That's why having you in our pack and mated to our alpha would give us hope—that one day it could happen for us."

I grabbed her hand. "It will happen. I have faith."

"Good, because everyone believes in you. They think you are the beginning to it all." Opening the car door, she got out and waved for me to follow.

I didn't know anything about the old magic, but I was sure as hell going to find out.

FIVE

BAILEY

"Do you want to go with me again tomorrow?" Tyla offered.

I stopped at the first step to Ryker's house and turned around, a huge smile on my face. "You don't think Blake will mind?"

She snorted. "Of course not. He enjoys watching me prance around in my short shorts while training the horses. I'll bring you a pair tomorrow." Then her gaze met something over my shoulder and I could feel Ryker approaching. "Or I'll just bring you a pair of baggy sweatpants. See ya tomorrow, B." As fast as she could, she sped out of the driveway, laughing the entire time.

"Did you have fun?" he asked.

I turned around and my heart thudded at the sight of him, dressed in a pair of ripped jeans and no shirt. "I did," I answered truthfully.

"What all did you do?"

Narrowing my gaze, I stalked up the steps. "Can't you just listen to my thoughts?"

He smirked. "I can, but I'd rather hear it from your mouth."

"Okay, let's see . . . she took me to eat lunch, and then we went to Blake's, where I got to ride the horses and watch Tyla train one." I walked inside and the smell from the kitchen was so heavenly, I moaned.

Ryker chuckled. "I'm glad you had a good day. You hungry?"

"I'm always hungry." I followed him into the kitchen and sat down at the table. There was food everywhere. "Did you cook this?"

He gestured for me to take the open chair across from him and sat down, cutting a bite of steak. "Yes."

"It looks amazing." I dug in and swallowed a bite of my own steak, savoring every minute of it. "Tastes good too."

"I've been on my own for many years, so I had to learn."

"Where's your family? Are they not a part of the pack?"

His jaw tensed. "They're dead."

"I'm sorry," I murmured, hating the guarded look in his eyes.

"Me too. I was just a child. It happened shortly after I met you."

I choked on my food and coughed. "How is that possible? Why don't I remember ever meeting you?"

He stared at me as he chewed, like he didn't know how to answer. "I tell you what . . . let's finish dinner, and then we'll talk all about it. You're going to need a drink, or ten."

I hurried with the rest of my meal. When I was done, he poured me a large glass of wine and ushered me to the couch. His hand brushed my side and the same electric current from before shot through my veins. It took my breath away.

"Don't worry, the same thing happens to me," he confessed, sitting beside me.

"Will it always be like that?"

"Not always. Only until we complete the bond. It's one of nature's ways of making sure we know who our mate is. What I want to know is, why didn't your parents tell you about true mates?"

"I don't know, but that's a damn good question. Tyla told me a little bit, but she left most of the explaining to you. She mentioned something about old magic."

Leaning over on his elbows, he looked down at his hands, and then over at mine. I could tell he wanted to touch me, but resisted. "It's called old magic because no one has seen it recently, except with me and you. There have been a handful of wolves over the past few decades who've found their true mates, but it's not common. The first time I met you, I was ten years old, which would've made you around seven. You had gotten lost in the woods and stumbled your way into our territory. You were scared and upset, so I brought you back to my pack and we watched over you for a time."

I put a hand over my mouth. "You lived in Canada? Can you tell me why I don't remember this? Surely I would've remembered meeting you."

"That's what I thought too when I came to your school. When you stayed away from me, I knew something was wrong. Someone must've erased your memories."

"And I don't remember our second meeting either. None of it makes any sense. I didn't even know there was another white wolf pack other than mine and the Yukon's."

He lifted his gaze to mine. "There's not. I was part of the Yukon pack, until my family was banished. I never found out why because on the way out of Canada my mother and I were attacked and she was murdered. My father was killed before we even left. I barely escaped, but I crossed the border into the states and was saved by another wolf pack who took me in."

"And now you're their alpha."

He nodded. "And you will be too . . . as my mate. Surely, you have no doubts about that, right? The signs are all there. I think I've proved them to you. You can't deny you feel it, can you?"

"I'm not going to lie, I feel things when you're around, but I have choices too. I'm not just going to spread my legs because I get all tingly when you touch me."

His lips spread into a mischievous smile. "Tingly, huh?"

"Get over yourself," I said, rolling my eyes. "What I do want to know is, how you can hear my thoughts but I can't hear yours? I don't like that."

"Don't worry, it won't stay that way for long. As soon as you taste my blood, you'll be linked to me and be able to hear whatever the hell you want."

"How did you get a taste of my blood? I don't remember offering up a vein."

Sighing, he bit his lip and licked it, as if he could still taste me on his tongue. "When I subdued you in the forest, I had to bite you to calm you down. At that point, I swallowed your blood and the connection opened. Did you not have any friends who were mated in your pack?"

I shook my head, lowering my gaze. "No, all of my friends were human, except Sebastian, the one who was with me the day I left college. Everyone else stayed away from me like they were afraid, or maybe even told to. I'm not sure. I don't know why my parents didn't tell me any of this."

"I'd like to know too. The legend of mates is more like a

folktale of sorts, a bedtime story; except everything about it is true. The magic of the wolf binds us to the moon, and also to our other half. Obviously, the first sign of finding your mate is that feeling in your gut which draws you to the other, almost like magnets. It's stronger in the males. The need to claim can be almost unbearable. That's why we're more violent the older we get without a mate. Did you feel me close by?"

I nodded. "All the time, but I just thought you were a rogue. What else happens when you meet your mate?"

He paused and cleared his throat. "I'm sure you remember the visions?"

My heart sped and my body tightened between my legs. I crossed them to help suppress the ache. "Are the visions always like that?"

"No. From what I've heard, they vary. Sometimes they'll be from a hundred years in the future, where you're holding your grandkids, or ones like ours that were recent."

"Does that make a difference?"

He closed his eyes, releasing a heavy sigh. "It does."

"What does it mean?"

"Visions can always change though, depending on the choices we make."

"What aren't you telling me?"

He smiled, but it didn't reach his eyes, hesitating before responding. "You read me well, angel. If you want to know the truth, usually when the visions aren't of our extended future, it means something will separate us; whether it be running away, death, or another tragedy."

"Or someone else," I whispered.

His temper spiked, his eyes flashing green. "That's not going to happen. No one will take you away from me. Again, the visions can change. The future isn't always set."

"How many times do the visions occur?"

"Every time blood is exchanged. The females are usually the ones who experience them, but the males see them through the bond."

I leaned my head against the couch. "I see. So if we want to know our future, we just have to bite each other. How messed up is that? Not to mention you can control my emotions."

Ryker moved closer. "It's used to help the other, not control them. I've deliberately not tried to calm you down because I know you don't like it. Believe me, it hasn't been easy. But as far as the biting, I think we could both enjoy that."

I elbowed him in the side. "Not if I'm biting off your ear."

He chuckled. "You can't hide the truth from me, angel."

I'd never bitten another wolf out of pleasure, only pain. I was curious to know what it'd be like, drinking his blood and feeling him inside me. The vision said it all though; we would complete the bond, even if it was short-lived. Gazing out the window, the sky was gray, with sheets of snow blanketing the ground and mountains in the distance. It was beautiful, but I knew I couldn't stay there, even if Ryker was my mate. Eventually, I would be hunted down and I couldn't bring that kind of war to him and his pack.

"All I want was to be normal, to live my life by my own choices, making my own decisions. What's the point of being an alpha if I can't do that?"

Turning my face toward him, he looked straight into my eyes. "You do have choices, Bailey. I'm not going to make them for you, unless I absolutely have to. You're my equal and I know that." He moved closer, his lips so close to mine.

I didn't even want to move away. "However, I can't promise I won't be the alpha in the bedroom."

I leaned into his touch and let him comfort me. "If we complete the bond, will I be able to alter your emotions as well?"

"Yes. But I'm not in a hurry. Right now your mind is everywhere, you're not ready. I only want you to come to me when you're absolutely sure this is what you want." He brushed the hair off my face, placing his forehead to mine. "We have time."

Sighing, I held onto his hands and closed my eyes before pulling them away. Why couldn't my life be simple? With furrowed brows, he stared down at me with those emerald green eyes of his. I couldn't believe the amount of power coming off of him; it was exhilarating and more powerful than any other alpha I'd encountered. My wolf stirred and I knew what she was thinking. *Mine*.

I swallowed hard, dreading my next words. "There's something I need to tell you."

"What is it?"

Taking a deep breath, I let it out slowly, lowering my gaze to the fists clutched in my lap. "I was never happy with my pack. I always dreamt of something more—something *else* for my life. When they let me go to school, it was the best time in my life. But my parents had made me promise that when I turned twenty-three, I would come back to the pack and fulfill my duties. I was willing to do that; at least until a week ago."

His body tensed. "What happened?"

"My parents had promised me to another wolf. The day I ran away was the day he came to claim me."

Eyes glowing, Ryker growled and his fangs lengthened, but he drew them back. "They promised you to someone who wasn't your mate? Why the fuck would they do that?"

I shrugged. "I don't know. I haven't spoken to them since I left. I kept running until I found my way here."

Taking my face in his hands, he tilted my chin, demanding I look at him. I knew he was trying to see into my mind, but I couldn't let him. With as much force as I could muster, I envisioned a wall to block him out, just to see if it could work. Thankfully, it did. I could feel him attempting to penetrate through, but with no success. "What aren't you telling me, Bailey? You can't keep me out forever. That kind of power only lasts for so long."

He was right. "It's not easy to talk about. I don't even know where to begin."

"How about the beginning? If you can't speak it, show it to me. Don't make me force my way into your mind. I'll do it if I have to."

Judging by the heated look in his eyes, he would do it. "Fine, I'll let you in. Then maybe you'll understand why I can't stay here." Reluctantly, I closed my eyes and let the memories of the night with Kade flood my mind. Everything from the beginning when he tried to claim me, to the part where I ripped out his throat.

Trembling with rage, Ryker was close to shifting, but he held it back. If we were bonded I could help control his wolf, but at this point, there was nothing I could do.

"Ryker, look at me." His eyes flashed and his fangs lengthened again. "I'm sorry. I didn't want you to know, but that's what happened. Now you see why I can't stay here. I *will* be found and there *will* be a war. I don't want you in the middle of it."

He growled low, his voice more animal than human. "It's too late." Getting to his feet, he stormed toward the front door and kicked it open, sliding his jeans and boxers to the floor. The magic began to shimmer around his body, but disappeared when I spoke.

"You're not a part of this fight, I am!" I shouted.

He turned to look at me, his gaze heated and full of rage. "You are my mate, and he had no right to fucking claim you. If his pack comes for you, they will have to get through me first."

"I can protect myself. I'm an alpha and just as strong as any of them."

"That's not the problem." He rushed down the front steps toward the woods.

"Then what is?" I shouted, going after him.

He paused and turned around, his shoulders rising and falling with his rapid breaths. "Kade was my brother, Bailey."

I gasped and watched him shift into his wolf before disappearing into the woods. How could someone like him be related to a sadistic bastard like Kade? I had just shown him images of ripping his brother's throat out. What the hell was I going to do now?

SIX

BAILEY

My first instinct was to chase after him, and if there was one thing I'd learned in life, it was to always trust my instincts. Shedding my clothes, I rushed out into the snow and shifted as I ran. Ryker's trail was strong, and even more so because he was enraged. An angry alpha was a deadly one. Up ahead, Ryker slowed his pace and I finally caught up to him, approaching slowly.

"Ryker, please shift back so we can talk. I wish I could apologize for killing your brother, but I can't."

His eyes glowed and he bared his fangs. Since I hadn't taken his blood yet, I wouldn't be able to hear him if he spoke. He stared at me before the magic swirled around his body, turning him into his human form.

"I don't want a goddamn apology. I should've been the one to kill him."

"So you're not mad at me?"

Breathing hard, he closed his eyes and knelt down on the snow in front of me, clenching his teeth. "No, I'm not mad at you. I saw what my brother did, and he deserved much more than he got. It kills me I wasn't there to protect you."

"I can take care of myself."

"I know."

"Why did you run off?"

He moved closer to me, putting his hands in my fur. "I'm pissed, Bailey. Watching your mate almost get raped by your brother isn't exactly a walk in the park. All I could see was red. If you hadn't ripped out his fucking throat, I would be halfway up to Canada by now."

Closing my eyes, I let the magic take over my body so I could shift back. When I did, Ryker pushed me back and rolled us onto our sides. His hands went to my face and he kissed me, opening my lips with his tongue. I pulled away, even though I didn't want to.

Breathing hard, he rested his forehead to mine. "I've wanted to do that since the first moment I saw you."

I couldn't deny it felt amazing. In fact, all I could think about was how good it was going to feel to let him claim me. Chest rumbling, his body reacted to my thoughts. My wolf wanted to mate, but the logical side of me wasn't ready. "What would've happened if Kade and I had . . ."

"Fucked?" he finished for me, wrapping me in his warm embrace.

I nodded. "You never told me what happens to those who end up mating with the wrong person."

Sighing, he leaned his chin down on the top of my head and placed his hand on my bare hip. The more he touched me, the more I wanted. It didn't help when he rubbed his rock hard arousal against my hip.

"Being forced to mate with another wolf is forbidden; it's punishable by death. If your parents came down here looking for you, I could legally kill them."

"No," I growled, trying to move out of his arms but he held me firm.

"Calm down, I'm not going to kill them. But I do hope they think twice before coming down here."

"I don't think it's them you should worry about. The Yukon pack will be the ones who'll want to avenge Kade's death."

"Then they'll be surprised when they find me." He gave me a humorless grin. "Back to your question, if you and Kade had mated, it'd feel like a part of you was missing. That's what it's like when you mate with the wrong person. You're not ever fully happy. Some wolves are okay with that and find whatever happiness they can in others, while some of us wait an entire lifetime, refusing to be with anyone other than their true mate."

"And when the need to mate drives you mad, how does that affect the older males? In my pack, I saw a lot of violence, but Sebastian made sure to keep me away from everyone."

His haunted gaze stared wearily down at me. "They can let out their frustrations by fucking human women. It appeases them for a time, but there's always a need there that never gets satisfied. Eventually, it gets to the point where something has to be done."

"Like what?" I asked, already knowing the answer by the look on his face.

"Putting them down. There are times when the wolves ask their pack to kill them. Those are always the hardest. I hope I never have to go through that again."

"Who was he?"

A sad smile splayed across his lips. "Odolf. He was a good man too."

"I'm sorry. I know that couldn't have been easy. To be

one of the strongest wolves in my pack, I don't know shit about them. If my parents had their way, I'd still be in Canada with Kade, plotting every single way I could kill him. I need to know why my parents kept me in the dark. There's something I'm missing."

Ryker held me tighter and lifted one of my legs so he could drape it over his. "If my parents were still alive, I bet they would know. My banishment has to be a part of it somehow. Kade was allowed to stay behind and I never understood why. It can't be a coincidence. I never spoke to him after we left, not even after all of these years. For all I know, he thought I was dead."

Visions of Kade swam through my mind. "Promise me you're nothing like him."

Tilting my chin up with his finger, he kissed the tip of my nose. "*That* I can promise. But if you don't believe me, take my blood. You'll feel everything I do, and our minds will be connected." He leaned down and kissed me gently on the lips. "The full moon isn't until another three weeks. I'll wait as long as you need me to."

Ryker slid his fingers along my neck, on down to my collarbone, making me tighten in all the right places. He tensed, growling low in his chest, sensing my excitement. It probably didn't help that my heart pounded out of control.

"My wolf is ready for it all, but I'll need answers before I can take that final step. The thought of biting you though . . ." I sniffed his neck and bit my lip, "excites me."

What I was about to do was going to either be the best or stupidest thing I'd ever done. Taking Ryker's blood felt right, just like the moon in the night sky. My wolf knew what it wanted, what it needed . . . and I was going to take it.

Opening my lips, I took a deep breath and lowered

them to his, grasping his face with my hands. His arms snaked around my waist and pulled me firmly into his body. Growling low, he twisted so that he covered me, burying me into the warm grass and mud—where our body heat had melted all of the snow.

"Let me taste you," I murmured.

Spreading my legs with his knee, he rubbed my clit with the tip of his cock. "Then do it, angel."

I allowed my fangs to lengthen and found his lips again, but he forced his tongue inside, slicing it across my teeth. Warm blood flowed down my throat. Almost immediately, everything changed. I could see things, feel things that weren't coming from my own body. The link was open.

"Can you feel me inside of you?" he asked silently.

"Yes."

"What do you want to see?"

"Everything."

Opening his mind, he let me see the past, the time when he found me alone in the woods. It was so long ago, I barely recognized myself. I was dressed in a little pink sundress, my blonde hair in pigtails, and I was so dirty it looked as if I'd been in the woods for days. Closing my eyes, I tried to think back to that time, but there was only a black hole from that age and younger. It was almost as if it was erased from my memory somehow.

"Why don't I remember you? I should be able to remember that time in my life."

He furrowed his brows. "I don't know. When I introduce you to the pack, I'll get Seraphina to work her magic on you. She'll be able to figure out something."

"Who's Seraphina?"

"She's one of the pack elders and very wise. I was hoping she'd help me find out why my family was banished, but she couldn't. Hopefully, she'll have more luck with you."

My skin tingled where his hands caressed me, and I didn't even want to stop him when he cupped my breasts. His fingers traced over my nipples and my whole body throbbed in anticipation. "You know this is dangerous. If you keep letting me touch you, I won't be able to control myself."

"Then why do you keep touching me?"

His eyes changed to that of his wolf. "I can't help it."

Lowering his lips to my breasts, he sucked on my nipple and bit down, drawing blood. I gasped and arched my back as he licked the blood away. Then, I was sucked into a vision.

"Angel, where are you?" Ryker calls.

I hide behind a tree, snickering, with a snowball in my hands. He steadily approaches, and I peek around the trunk. He hasn't found me yet, but he has a sly grin on his face as if he thinks he's going to fool me. Before he could attack, I attack first, throwing the snowball right at his head. He falls to the ground, laughing.

"You're gonna regret that."

I stood there, smirking, with my hands on my hips. "Don't think so. I'm not afraid of the big, bad wolf."

"We'll see about that." He jumps to his feet and chases after me, and all I could do was laugh. It slowed me down, but I wanted to get caught. We're running through the trees out in the middle of nowhere, with only our footprints in the snow. It's not long before Ryker lunges and we go tumbling down to the ground. Chuckling, he pins me down.

"I let you catch me," I say to him.

He smirks. "You would've tired out eventually. We both know I'm stronger."

"Want to put that to the test? I'll fight you, right here and now."

Brushing his thumb across my lips, he leans closer, smiling. "So stubborn. You said the same thing to me when we were kids. I wish you could remember. We used to play out by the lake and ice skate. Every time you would fall, I'd laugh. It used to piss you off."

"Please tell me I kicked your ass after that." I don't remember those times, but I long to get those memories back. One way or another, it's going to happen.

He shakes his head, smile growing wider. "Nope, but you did break the ice and I fell through."

"Serves you right."

"You weren't saying that when I never resurfaced."

My smile disappears. "What happened?"

"Nothing bad, just playing a little joke on you. I heard you screaming my name and then watched you jump in the water to save me. You were so young and small, there was no way you could've gotten me out of the water. It was then when I knew something had changed. I had the overwhelming sense to protect you. When you couldn't find me in the water, you panicked. I ended up rescuing you and getting you out. I felt horrible for playing the joke on you."

"You knew I was your mate back then?"

"I'm not really sure what I knew, but I knew you were special. Mine to protect."

"And what do you know now?" I ask.

Cupping my cheek, he leans down and kisses me, long and deep. He pulls back and gazes down at me. "I know that whatever happens, I'll protect you no matter the cost, mated or not. I love you."

I look up at him and smile. "I love you too."

"Bailey!" Gasping, I woke up from the vision with

Ryker staring straight down at me, his gaze concerned. "Did you have a vision?"

I nodded. "You didn't see it did you?"

"Something held me back. Was it you?"

"Not that I know of, or at least not consciously."

"What was it about?"

I closed my eyes and remembered every second of it, only giving him images from it. "I guess you'll have to find out when it happens," I teased.

He bit my lip. "Fine, but while you were out, take a look at this." He traced his finger over my nipple where he had drawn blood just a few short minutes earlier. The wound had completely healed.

"Wow, do all mated couples have this ability?" I asked.

He shook his head. "No, that's something completely new. If just bonding through blood makes us this strong, imagine how powerful we'll be when we actually complete it." Biting his lip, he slid his fingers up my thigh and I shivered. Chuckling, he gazed down at me, his wolf eyes shining through. "I know you don't want to move too fast, but we can always give our wolves a taste of what they want."

Opening my legs, I smiled. "Oh yeah, like what?" My hand traced down his body, to the V of his lower abs.

He pushed his hand between us and rubbed a thumb over my clit before pushing a finger inside. "Like this."

I moaned. "But what about this?" My fingers found his cock and I stroked him, squeezing the tip on each upstroke.

He swore out loud and thrust his hips into my grip. "We wouldn't want to disappoint our wolves, now would we?" I shook my head, unable to respond, and he lowered his lips to my breasts. Sucking on my nipples, he went back and forth between them both. My thighs were drenched, growing wetter as my release drew near. I could feel it building more and more the harder he pushed inside of me.

Our hips moved against one another in time with our hands. When I was close, I pulled his fingers out of me and brought them to my mouth. Sucking on his fingers, I looked deep into his eyes and rocked my clit up and down the length of his shaft. Pushing against one another, I gave into the need, screaming out his name as I trembled. His abs jerked and spasmed as he coated our stomachs with his release.

His dark chuckle echoed in my ear and I could feel his warm breath tickling my neck as he kissed me. "I love hearing my name on your lips."

Pushing him over, I sat on him and looked down. "Next time, I'm on top."

SEVEN

RYKER

"Take this," I said, handing Bailey one of my credit cards.

Sitting up, she rubbed her eyes and took it. "What's this for?"

I glanced down at her bare chest and then over to her one set of clothes on the floor. "I think you need more clothes. Don't get me wrong, looking at you is nice, but I can't have you meeting the pack naked."

She giggled. "Probably not. Did you sleep okay?"

"It wasn't too bad." After our time in the woods, we came back and I let her have my bedroom while I slept in one of the spare ones. The temptation to fully claim her was too strong to even consider sleeping next to her.

"Thank you for letting me have your bed. You could've slept in here with me."

"Trust me, there would have been no sleep going on." Grabbing my ranger hat off the dresser, I turned and started for the door. "There's plenty to eat downstairs. I'll be back this afternoon. And don't worry about the limit on the card. Buy whatever clothes you want." Opening the bedroom door, I glanced over my shoulder at her. She nodded, her gaze troubled. "What's wrong?"

She held up the card. "I have my own money . . . I just don't have access to it right now. After what happened with Kade, I had to get out of there fast. I left everything behind. I don't even have my license."

"And if you brought that stuff with you, you would've been easier to track."

She groaned. "So basically, I can't do anything with my life."

"Not yet, but you'll get it all back. Blake will be able to help us. He can get your license, bank records, everything. He can even make you untraceable."

"He's that good at undercover work?"

"One of the best. I'll talk to him about it next weekend. Every Saturday, the guys all get together at the local bar for drinks. Tyla will be there too."

"Is she the one taking me shopping?"

I nodded. "Texted her this morning. She'll be here in an hour."

She slid out of bed and reached for the clothes on the floor. "When will I meet the rest of your pack?"

"Our pack," I corrected. "It's our pack now. And you'll meet them tomorrow. Tonight we're going to have some fun." I made my way down the stairs and called up to her, "Have fun with Tyla."

"I'm sure I will," she said before I walked out.

Cedric waited for me by my truck, dressed in his ranger uniform. "Any news?" I asked.

"None. So far, the perimeter is clear. There hasn't been anyone close to the border."

"Good, let's hope it stays that way." We both got in my

truck and started down the gravel driveway toward the main road.

"How's it going? From what I can tell, she's a real spitfire."

"You have no fucking idea." By the sly look on his face, I knew what he wanted to ask next. "And no, I haven't fucked her if that's what you wanted to know."

Chuckling, he held up his hands. "Hey, I was just curious. We've heard so many stories, I had to see if any were true. How many times did you have to jack off?"

"Probably not as much as you do every day, cocksucker."

For the twenty minutes it took to drive to the station, I told him about Bailey taking my blood and what it was like. Apparently, the rest of the pack was curious as well. I could only hope our union would bring the magic back.

THE TRAILS WERE STILL COVERED in snow and would be until midsummer. Being able to work in the forests was one of the perks of being a ranger. I also wasn't scared of running into bears like most of my coworkers. That was why Cedric and I always went to the deepest parts of the trails to inspect them before tourist season started.

"Anything up that way?" Cedric shouted. He stayed behind to clear off some broken limbs that had fallen from the trees above.

Glancing up ahead, there was a medium sized tree across the trail. "Yeah, but I got it. Stay where you are." With our wolf strength, there hadn't been a job on the trail I couldn't handle. It didn't take long to break the tree down and clear the trail.

"Do we have time to go further up?" Cedric asked, appearing over the rocky slope.

I looked at my watch. "Not today. We can finish up tomorrow."

He hopped off the rocks onto the trail. "Sounds good to me. I could use a beer or twelve. Maybe even a night with Samantha." Samantha was one of the waitresses at the bar, and one of his many conquests. One thing about being a wolf was that we couldn't procreate with humans. If we could, Cedric would have over a hundred kids by now.

"Have fun with that. I'm pretty sure she slept with Emmett last weekend. It's a good thing we don't contract diseases."

He guffawed. "Got that right. But I don't give a shit who she fucks. She can suck a dick like a champ."

Thoughts of Bailey ran through my mind and then I could feel her, poking around. *"Are you spying on me?"* I asked her.

"No, I was curious to see if distance played a factor in our connection. You know, like a cell phone if it's out of range, it doesn't work. How far away are you?"

"That depends, where are you?"

"I'm at Blake's, getting ready to ride Nightshade."

"Ah, letting another male between your legs. I'm jealous."

"You should be, he's a stallion."

"Is Tyla riding with you?"

"No, she's staying behind. One of Blake's friends from North Carolina is here. Tyla thinks he's hot. It wouldn't surprise me if she asks you if she can turn him."

I groaned, making Cedric look at me like I'd lost my mind.

"What's wrong?" he asked.

"Nothing, just talking to Bailey." Then to her I said, *"Tyla can ask all she wants, she's not turning Blake or any of his friends. She can wait for her true mate, like everyone else."*

I could hear her laughing in my mind. *"She knows. I think she does it to get a rise out of you."*

"A giant pain in my ass is what she is." Tyla was a loyal wolf and a good friend. She was one of the only females in the pack who hadn't tried to get me to mate them.

Bailey growled in my mind. *"I heard that. Surely they know about me and have backed the fuck off, right?"*

"Well, angel, until you're ready to mate with me, I'm technically fair game."

"Then so am I." The connection went silent.

"I think I just pissed her off." I chuckled, glancing at Cedric.

"I have no doubt. If I ever find my mate, she's going to spend a great deal of time hating me; especially if she finds out how many women I've fucked. Does Bailey know about you?"

I knew what he was asking and I made sure to keep that part of my mind hidden away. "No, but I'm pretty sure she doesn't want to know how many women I've been with. Just like I don't care to know the details about the men she's fucked."

We were almost off the trail when my phone rang. I thought it was going to be Tyla, but it was Ian Randale, alpha of the Northwestern pack. "Ian, what's going on, my man?"

"Nothing good. You have a problem heading your way."

"Fuck me, are you serious?" I already knew what was going on.

"Dead serious. It was three wolves, asking if I'd seen a

female Arctic wolf. When I asked why, they said it was pack business. Obviously, they didn't get a scent of her so they left. I don't know if they're headed your way, but be prepared. They're on the hunt."

"Thanks for the heads up. I'll inform my pack." I hung up and immediately dialed Tyla's number.

"What are you going to do?" Cedric asked.

"Something that'll piss Bailey off if she finds out."

"Then I suggest you not think about it."

I waited for Tyla to answer her phone. "Easier said than done, my friend. You'll find out one of these days."

"Hey, what's up," she answered.

"Where's Bailey?"

"Out riding, why?"

"Keep your eye on her. Ian called and said there were some wolves looking for her."

"Okay, I won't let her out of my sight. Are you going to tell her?"

"No. If I do, she'll try to leave. Just act normal and we'll do everything as planned. Tonight we'll go out to the bar, tomorrow I'll let her meet the pack, and then I'm taking her somewhere safe."

"You're leaving?"

"Only until the enemies pass us by."

"We could always hide her so you don't have to leave."

"I wish we could, but it's not going to work." Not everyone knew why Bailey had come to us and if they did, they'd realize the greater threat.

"Why not?"

"Because . . . I know the wolves coming after Bailey."

"How?"

"I used to be a part of their pack."

EIGHT

BAILEY

"Thanks for letting me ride Nightshade," I said to Blake.

He smiled and fetched a bucket of water from the hose. He'd told me all about how he grew up a city slicker and how Ryker and Tyla turned him into a cowboy. The stories of his undercover missions were amazing. Even though he wasn't a shifter, he was one lethal human.

"He likes beautiful women riding him."

Nightshade bumped me with his nose and I laughed. "I've never ridden a horse before."

"Really? You look like a natural out there."

"All right, Evans, no flirting with Ryker's woman. He'll skin you alive," Tyla teased. Blake's friend, Wyatt Erickson, walked in beside her. They'd been inseparable since we showed up. He was a good looking man, dressed in a pair of jeans, a polo shirt, with his light brown hair in messy spikes.

Blake winked at her. "I'm not scared. I'm sure his bark is worse than his bite." We tried to hide our giggles at the comment and he looked sideways at us before continuing. "You gonna dance with me tonight?"

She smirked. "Maybe, if you buy me a drink."

He leaned closer to me. "Why is she always so difficult?"

"Because I can be," she replied, reaching for my hand. "And right now, I need to get this one home so she can get ready for the night."

I scratched Nightshade's ear and nuzzled him. "See you tomorrow, boy. That is, if it's okay," I said, glancing over at Blake.

"Come anytime. You're always welcome. Wyatt and I will see you both tonight."

Tyla and I said our goodbyes and got in her car. "What's up with you and Wyatt?" I asked as we drove away.

She batted her eyelashes innocently. "Just some friendly flirting. He's not exactly my type, but he sure is easy on the eyes."

"So is Ryker. He told me you were the only one in the pack who hasn't tried to get him to mate with you."

"Oh hell, he told you that?"

"Is it true?"

She sighed. "Yes, but nothing ever happened. He never slept with any of them or promised them anything."

"Will any of them try to challenge me?"

Eyes wide, she burst out in laughter. "Are you kidding me? They'd be stupid if they did that. Any wolf from a mile away could feel your power. I don't plan on ever getting on your bad side."

That was good to know.

She dropped me off at Ryker's house just in time for him to pull up and see the several shopping bags in my hand. He got out of the car, followed by another wolf who was dressed in the same ranger uniform. He had dark blond hair and a smirk on his face; he was one of the six who kept watch over me.

"Bailey, this is Cedric, my second in command."

I held out my hand. "Yes, I recognize the smirk."

Cedric took my hand, roaring in laughter. "I guess you're saying I look like my wolf?"

Ryker narrowed his gaze, studying Cedric's face. "You're right. He does."

"Only the smile," I added. "I remember it getting bigger when I sat out on the front porch, waiting for everyone to leave. I wanted to smack it off your face."

"I'm sure that would've been quite interesting," Cedric replied.

Ryker laughed. "If by interesting, you mean watching you run home with your tail between your legs . . . then yes."

"Okay, if you two are done bashing me, I'm going to change clothes and meet you at the bar."

I watched him walk past the house to another one on the other side of the field. "Does he live here too?"

Ryker's arm brushed mine as he stood beside me. "He does. That's his cabin out there. Some of the men in the pack are builders. They built everything you see here." On Ryker's land, there was the main ranch, a smaller cabin and two separate barns.

"Very nice. It looks like you have a lot of talent in your pack."

"Our pack. And yes, we do." He turned to face me. "Are you still mad at me?"

"I am," I replied, crossing my arms over my chest.

He grinned. "Good. You're sexy when you're angry."

"And you're annoying."

"Well, I'm probably about to annoy you even more. After you meet the pack tomorrow, we're leaving."

"Where to?"

"Somewhere safe, where no one can find you. If the Yukon pack comes, they'll see you're not here and move on. As soon as the threat's gone, we can come back."

"How am I going to travel? I don't have anything to prove my identity."

Taking my bags, he started for the door and I followed. "That's why I'm going to talk to Blake tonight. He'll help us out. Cedric will fill in as alpha if anyone were to come looking for you."

"I can go on my own. You shouldn't leave your pack," I argued.

"And you need to stop being so stubborn. I thought you were adventurous. You can even pick the place you want to go. This is your chance to see more of the world. You're not scared are you?" He was goading me.

I could hear the laughter inside his head, but I could also feel his hesitance. Something was wrong. "I'm not scared."

"Then prove it," he countered with a sly grin.

I stalked up to him, my body flush with his. "I will, even though I know you're hiding something." He looked to the side and I decided to let it go for now. "I know exactly where I want to go first."

NINE

BAILEY

Ryker fumbled around in the kitchen, and I smelled eggs and bacon coming through the bedroom door. I rolled over and stared at the far wall. I thought for sure he would sleep with me last night, but he didn't; he only kissed me goodnight. At the bar, he'd spent most of the night talking to Blake, trying to get his help on my situation, while I talked to Cedric and the other guys in the pack.

"You're disappointed I didn't sleep with you last night?" Ryker asked.

"Not at all. I enjoy sleeping alone. I have more room."

"You lie, angel. I could feel your disappointment this morning. All you have to do is tell me you want me and I'll stay. I have to hear it."

"You know I want you, Ryker. I'm sure you could figure that out the other night."

My whole life, I never needed anyone to protect me, not even my parents. And when it came down to it, they didn't do a very good job when it came to Kade. I knew I could survive on my own. Admitting I needed or even wanted someone was foreign to me. Saying the words out loud was near impossible.

"You showed me, but haven't told me. Words can be powerful," he replied.

Rolling my eyes, I got out of bed and threw on some clothes before going downstairs. He was in the kitchen with his back to me, shirt off, wearing only a pair of boxers. *Holy fuck.* "So if I take off my clothes and lay down on the table, you wouldn't have sex with me?"

He chuckled. "Nope."

"You sure?"

"Yep." He continued on with cooking while I stood there, dumbfounded. I didn't believe him for a second. His back stiffened when I took off my shirt and pants and climbed up on the table.

"I am so hungry," I announced, waiting for him to turn around. When he did, he completely ignored me and sat down with his plate of food.

He pointed to the counter. "Your plate's up there."

"You're seriously not going to look at me?"

He studied an invisible spot on the table and placed a piece of bacon in his mouth, crunching it slowly. "You're not ready for that."

I waited for him to sneak a peek but he didn't. "Who's the stubborn one now?"

He chuckled. "Still you, sweetheart. You have me beat."

Fetching the clothes off the floor, I slid them on and grabbed my plate of food. He had more willpower than I gave him credit for. By the smirk on his face, he heard my thoughts. *Cheeky bastard.*

"How's your breakfast?"

I scooped a forkful of eggs into my mouth. "It's good. How did you learn to cook?"

"Seraphina made sure to teach me when I was a boy. She's the one who took me in. It was either learn or catch my food in the wild." He finished his food and lifted his gaze to mine. It was so hard to turn away from those eyes.

"Do you miss your family?"

He smiled, but it was sad. "Every day. I just wish I had answers."

I nodded, trying hard not to let the thoughts of what happened to mine run through my mind. "I miss mine too, even though they betrayed me. I have no idea what's going on up there, or what happened after I left. I don't even know if they're okay."

He reached for my hand. "You don't need to worry about that now. They literally threw you to the wolves. You'll get to meet Seraphina today. I'm interested to see what she says about you."

He had a point about my parents, but I still loved them. If Seraphina could shed some light on what happened, I was all up for it. "What time will everyone be here?" I asked.

Taking my empty plate, he put our dishes in the sink. "A couple of hours. Blake should be here soon with your paperwork. We're leaving tonight."

"And are you sure it's a good idea to leave the pack?" I got up and helped him clean the kitchen. I didn't know much about his people, but if the Yukon pack had murdered his family, I highly doubted they'd care about others.

Taking my hands, Ryker turned me to face him. "They'll be fine. They're a strong lot. But it's good to see you care about them."

"I care about the well-being of all wolves, except for your brother. I'd never known anyone to be so cruel."

He pulled me to him and I laid my head against him,

listening to the calming sound of his heart beating in his powerful chest. "Kade wasn't always that way. My uncle was the cruel one in the pack; he was our alpha. If my brother learned from him, it doesn't surprise me he changed over the years."

"Do you have any other siblings?"

He shook his head. "Just Kade."

"I'm sorry," I whispered. "I know it can't be easy to be betrayed like that." Taking his face in my hands, I kissed him gently. It started out soft, but then he deepened it, gripping my waist to bring me closer. I could feel the need inside him, tearing him apart. His wolf wanted to claim me, but he fought against it.

Pulling away from the kiss, I looked into his glowing gaze. "How long can you fight it?"

For a brief second, his wolf eyes flashed through. "For as long as I need to."

I leaned up to kiss him again, but a knock at the door interrupted us. I recognized Blake's scent almost immediately.

"Why don't you take your shower and get packed up. There are plenty of suitcases in my closet to choose from."

"What time does our flight leave?" I started for the stairs and he to the door.

"Six. We'll leave for the airport directly after the meeting."

"Okay. Tell Blake I said hi." I made my way up the stairs to the bedroom and shut the door. Blake and Ryker talked downstairs and I was shocked at how easily he was able to acquire my information. I guess he was as good as they said.

"Are you nervous?"

I looked out the window at all the cars before answering Tyla. "A little. I can't help but wonder how they'll take me. My own pack treated me as if I was a leper, except for Sebastian."

"Who's that?"

"My father's second in command and my protector. He was more my friend than anything. Or at least, I thought he was. He betrayed me in the end, just like my parents. I guess you can say my experience with other wolves hasn't been promising."

She sat beside me, bumping me in the shoulder. "We're going to be your family now, Bailey. Everyone downstairs will love and respect you as their alpha. You have to be willing to open up and give them a chance."

"I will. Everything just seems to be moving so fast."

"You're not having doubts are you?"

"No, of course not. It's just, I wish things could be simpler. I used to be so jealous of my friend from college. Knowing she'd be able to fall in love, get married, and do as she pleased. I envied her freedom."

"You'll be free here as well. As far as getting married, is that something you want? You know our kind don't exactly have weddings."

"I know, but I can always wish." I remembered back to when Becca and I would go to one of the dress stores and try on wedding gowns. It was silly, but I knew it was something I'd never get to experience.

Opening the bedroom door, Ryker slipped his head inside. "You ready, angel? Everyone's here."

Tyla put her arm around me. "You can do this. I'll see you downstairs." She squeezed my shoulder and then disappeared, leaving Ryker and I alone.

"So how many wolves are in your pack?" I asked him.

"*Our* pack," Ryker reminded me for the umpteenth time as he pulled me in for a kiss. "Why don't you go take a look?"

He opened the door wide and I held in my surprised gasp as we entered the living room. Dozens of men, women, and children all turned to gape at us. "Oh my God," I breathed. The sight was absolutely amazing. I had never known a pack to be so large.

There weren't just Arctic wolves either. There were reds, grays, and even a small number of Arctic wolves all congregated in one place, smiling at each other with *no* rivalry. I could feel the power of their blood calling to me, giving me strength. It was something I'd never felt before with my own pack.

"Do you feel that? I've never felt it before until now," Ryker mentioned through our bond.

"Me neither."

Taking my hand, Ryker walked me through the crowd, and I said my hellos to everyone as I passed. In the corner was a group of wolves that had immense power pouring off of them. When they saw us approaching, they bowed their heads. I had already gotten to know a few of them at the bar, including Cedric. I didn't realize how strong they were until they were all together.

"Everyone, this is Bailey Whitehill, my mate," he announced.

One by one they introduced themselves, but of course it was Cedric's smart ass mouth that caught my attention as he made his way toward us.

"Ready for the full moon," he quipped, punching Ryker in the arm. "The guys were wondering when he was ever going to catch you."

Ryker rolled his eyes and punched him back. "Yeah, well I would've liked to see you do any better. She wasn't exactly an easy girl to follow."

Cedric turned to me and grinned even wider. "On behalf of the pack, I want to thank you for getting him out of the shitty ass mood he's been in for the past year."

Lifting my brows, I glanced up at Ryker and smiled. "So basically, he's saying you've been a dick? I thought you could control yourself better than that, Mr. Alpha."

He leaned down, whispering in my ear. "You're one to talk, angel. I can feel the desire inside of you when you look at me. Trust me, it makes things *very* hard."

Cedric watched our interaction, clearly amused. "If you're done mind-fucking each other, I just wanted to officially welcome you to the pack and tell you that we're all happy you're here."

Nodding, I smiled and said, "Thank you." Knowing very well they weren't going to be too happy when we told them about the two packs most likely hunting me.

Ryker rubbed my back and sighed. "It's time."

Taking a deep breath, I let it out slowly and walked with him to the front of the room. Ryker walked up with confidence and it was the only thing that kept me going. He believed in his pack, and knew without a doubt they would stand by and protect me. I just didn't want to ask them to.

"You're not, angel . . . I am."

All eyes turned our way as Ryker cleared his throat, ready to make his announcement. It was amazing how so many different wolves were part of his pack, with an Arctic wolf as the alpha. Never in a million years would I have thought such a thing possible.

"As you all know," he began, "I spent the last five years watching over Bailey, and then some in the previous years.

When the time comes, she'll be your alpha as well. She didn't initially come here willingly. Through reasons I have yet to figure out, her family had promised her to another wolf, not telling her about the magic of mates. It turns out, that other wolf was my brother."

The energy in the room spiked as words of rage and disgust spewed from everyone's mouths. Questions were thrown at us, asking why my family would do that to me, but Ryker and I didn't have the answers. Instead, he held up his hands, signaling for silence.

"We don't know why her family didn't tell her about mate magic or why she was promised to Kade, but I do know that—"

"I know why," a voice called out.

The room fell silent as an elderly woman with long white hair and weathered skin approached the front wearing a white, silky robe. She was old, much older than any wolf I'd ever seen.

"Seraphina," Ryker replied in my mind.

Slowly, she waltzed up to us, keeping her solemn gaze on mine. My heart thundered in my chest, but Ryker grabbed my hand, and it calmed me. I wanted answers, but I had to admit, I was nervous about hearing them.

Ryker bowed his head out of respect. "Thanks for coming, Seraphina. As always, I am open to your wisdom."

Seraphina held out her hand to me. "Come, child. Take my hand."

Her crystal blue eyes were kind and gentle, but had a sadness behind them. I took her hand and she pulled me to her, holding on tight. Her eyes closed and she mumbled something under her breath. "Too many secrets and lies have befallen you. Especially from those you love." More mumbled words escaped her lips, and then out of nowhere, a spark of power radiated through the room and through me. Gasps erupted from the pack as it traveled through each and every one of them. The magic was familiar, like I had felt it before.

Before opening her eyes, she grinned. "My suspicions were right."

"What do you mean?" I asked, whispering the words.

Tears forming in her eyes, she lifted her hands to my face. "You're not a Whitehill. You, my child, are royal."

The crowd gasped, and when I looked at Ryker, he was wide-eyed in surprise. "I don't understand. Care to elaborate?"

"It means your bloodline is the most powerful of all wolves," Ryker explained.

Seraphina spoke up next. "He's right. You are from the direct line of ancient wolves who disappeared about three centuries ago. No one knows where they went or, until recently, if they were still alive. When they ruled, the packs were at peace, living in harmony with one another.

"Over the years, greed poisoned our magic and the packs slowly drifted apart, forming new alliances. Now that we're separated, the magic of the moon grows weaker. Our abilities to find our mates all but disappeared, making it harder for our wolves to find happiness. It is my belief, dear child, that you are the one who can help us."

"How is this possible? How can I fix the dying magic?"

She smiled and took my hands. "By sealing the bond with your one true mate. Ryker was born special too. Look around you." I did as she said and gazed at the people in his pack. "Over the years, he's brought all of these people together under one united front. No other alpha has the ability to do that anymore. It's how the royals led their people centuries ago. And when you complete the bond, your combined power will be the first step in setting the natural balance—to restore what we've lost."

One by one, the wolves in the room all dropped to their knees. Confusion swept over me. "I don't understand. How can my parents be Whitehill's and I'm not? Wouldn't they be royals as well?"

Ryker joined me, his gaze wary. "I don't think they are your biological parents, Bailey."

"What he says is true," Seraphina added. "I don't know how you ended up with them, but they aren't your family. If they were, they never would've promised you to Kade."

I couldn't even wrap my head around what she was saying. "How is that even possible? They're my parents. They're all I've known."

She nodded wearily. "I'm not saying they didn't love you. It's possible they were forced to do what they did."

Dread settled in the pit of my gut, the anger bubbling right underneath the surface. I didn't even know who I was anymore. "Why can't I remember any of my encounters with Ryker, or with my real family? It's all just a black hole when I try to think back."

She looked down at my hand, furrowing her brows. "They were wiped clean. When I touched you, I could feel the dark magic still binding itself to your memories, locking down your thoughts. Only a very powerful witch can do such a spell."

"But who?" Then I glared at Ryker. "Did you have a witch like that in the Yukon pack?"

Releasing a heavy sigh, he nodded. "Her name was Maret."

I felt violated, robbed. "How do I get them back?" I growled the words.

Seraphina hesitated for a moment. "The only way

would be if the witch willingly reversed the spell, or if you killed her."

"She took away the memories of my real family. One way or another, I'll get them back."

She sighed. "I know you want them back, but it's not worth risking your life to get them. Right now, your only concern should be staying safe until the full moon comes."

"Which is what I want to discuss with you all," Ryker announced, turning to the group. "If the Yukon pack is on the hunt, I have no doubt they'll come this way. If they see me with Bailey, there will surely be a fight. I don't want to bring that kind of war to your doorsteps. Bailey and I will be leaving tonight until the threat's passed. Cedric is my second in command; he'll make the decisions while we're gone."

"What if we're willing to fight?" one of the wolves asked. His name was Rafe, one of the wolves I met at the bar. He was tall and stout, a warrior at heart. I enjoyed talking to him about his building projects. I had no doubt he'd kick ass in a fight.

Ryker was about to answer, but I put my hand on his arm. *"Give me a second to speak."* I looked up at him and he nodded.

"If a fight is what they want, I'll give it to them. I'm the one who killed their alpha." The room fell silent. "My goal is to lead them away from you, from your children. I haven't been a part of your pack for long, but that doesn't take away from the fact I don't want to see anyone hurt because of me."

As if on command, men stood and formed a line in front of me. Cedric was first. He knelt down, bowing his head.

"What are you doing?" I whispered.

He chuckled and winked up at me. "Giving you my

life." Taking my hand, he held it in his. "I, Cedric Convel, give you my life, my honor, and my strength. I will fight and die for you, if you so choose it. You are my alpha." When he stood, he leaned down and whispered in my ear. "I've searched years for my mate and haven't found her. If you can restore the magic of the moon, I will forever be in your debt."

For the first time since I'd met him, he was completely serious. I nodded with confidence. "I will do everything within my power to see that it happens."

Completely in awe, yet numb, I stood there with Ryker by my side as one after the other pledged their allegiance to me. Everything I'd known to be true had been torn away from me in just one night. I was nothing to my old pack but a pawn in a game. Whatever they were playing, I was determined to win. One way or another, I was going to get my answers.

Once everyone had left, it was time to leave for the airport. Ryker took my hand and brought it to his lips. "Everything will be fine, angel. After we finish mating, we'll be stronger than any pack out there. You'll get your answers."

"I sure hope so. If we don't, I'm never going to know what happened to my real family, or who I really am."

"Even if you don't find out who you really are, there's one thing we know for certain. You're mine, as I am yours. We found each other, and now you have a new family, a new beginning."

"You're right. But something tells me it's not going to be so easy."

With his hand on the back of my neck, he pulled me to him and kissed me. "Nothing worth having ever is. Now let's go, we have a plane to catch." We loaded up the truck and started down the road. When we got to the airport, he unloaded the bags and locked up. "North Carolina, here we come."

Snickering, I grabbed my bag. "Blake said the beaches there were beautiful. And they aren't crowded like other places. Besides, I've never even seen an ocean before. It'll be a new experience."

He put his arm around me. "That it will. If all else fails, at least I'll get to see you in a bikini." I started to laugh, but then froze. "Bailey, what's wrong?"

For the briefest moment, I thought I'd felt the presence of another wolf, a strong one. But the feeling disappeared so fast I couldn't tell if I imagined it, or if I was just paranoid.

"Bailey!" Ryker shouted, grabbing my attention. I scanned the parking lot and didn't see a thing. "Are you okay?"

I nodded. "Yeah, of course. Let's go. I'm ready to see the beach."

TEN

BAILEY

"It's so beautiful." Seeing the ocean from the plane didn't compare to the way it actually felt to have the sand between my toes and smell the salty, sea air.

"You're beautiful," Ryker murmured. *"And sexy as hell in that bathing suit."*

I smiled, and turned around. "Thanks. You're not so bad yourself."

"Are you going to stand out here all night?"

The sky was turning dark, but I couldn't bring myself to leave. There was so much I'd missed in life, and I didn't want to miss another second of it. "I'm thinking about it." I laughed.

"Then I guess it's a good thing I brought dinner."

I turned to see he had a bottle of wine and a paper bag, with a towel draped over his bare shoulder. "How did I not know you left?"

He nodded toward the water. "You were mesmerized. Anyway, there's an Italian place down the street. I thought it looked promising. I know you like lasagna."

"And how do you know that?"

Setting the towel down, he pulled out our food and poured me a cup of wine. "You ate it at least three times a week when you were in college."

Eyes wide, I stood there in shock. "Creepy..."

He rolled his eyes. "I wasn't *always* watching you, Bailey. I still had the pack to look after too. But for the most part, I did keep tabs on you."

"Why, because I'm your mate?"

His gaze narrowed. "You forget I knew you before the word 'mate' even popped in my head. I'm the one who found you alone in the woods when we were kids. I never left your side the entire time you were with my pack." He passed me a takeout container of lasagna and my stomach rumbled.

I nodded, even though I couldn't remember. "I know, I'm sorry. With having only human friends, they had their boyfriends, fell in love, and got married. I thought that's what it would be like for me. That I'd get to pick someone of my choosing."

A deep growl rumbled in his chest. "You did choose me. Why do you think we were separated? We clearly showed signs of it early on. You were taken away and I was banished from the pack. I don't think that's a coincidence. Once you get your memories back, you'll see."

"Until then?" I asked.

His jaw tensed as he stabbed away at his food. "We get to know each other the real way, by talking. I can't make you love me, especially when you're fighting your instincts."

I didn't want to fight them, I just wanted to make my own choices. I knew deep down there was more to me and Ryker, but my whole life had been built on lies. I needed something tangible. "I know we have this connection to each other, but I want us to be together because of who we are, not because of magic. I want you to be with me because of me."

"What do you think I've done over the past five years? While you were away at school, I watched you every single day, learning all your likes and dislikes. Stalkerish or not, I had no choice. It was the only way I could be around you."

"Why didn't you try to talk to me?"

He huffed. "I wanted to, but I didn't want to draw any more attention than I already had. Your bodyguard was always around. I didn't want him to know I was there."

I choked on my wine. "Bodyguard? Who the hell are you talking about?"

"The wolf you left with that day I came for you," he said, finishing off the rest of his food.

Had he lost his mind? "Sebastian? He was only there to drop me off and bring me home. I would've known if he was there."

"Obviously, you didn't. He followed you everywhere."

Was I too engrossed in my freedom to even notice? "How can that be possible? I've always been able to sense other wolves when they're around."

He shrugged. "I don't know, but we need to add it to the long list of questions you have." Sighing, Ryker laid down on the sand, his gaze up at the sky. I could feel his emotions as if they were my own. He was worried about the pack, but his main concern was for me.

Rolling over on my side, I brushed my body against his, laying my head on his chest. It satisfied both our wolves when we were touching. "Ryker," I whispered. He turned his head, his brows lifting in response. I could get lost in those green eyes of his. "Will you do something for me?"

"Anything."

I reached over and clasped my hand with his, the

tingling sensation making me shiver. "Give me your memories. From the moment you first saw me, to the moment I left. I want to see what I'm missing."

His lips brushed my temple and he smiled. "Close your eyes."

ELEVEN

RYKER

My memories of Bailey were just as fresh as if they'd happened yesterday. I showed her everything, even the times when Kade would come along on our adventures through the woods. He didn't like that she chose me over him. Reliving the past made me realize the betrayal of my pack went deeper than I imagined.

"I didn't realize we were so close," she whispered, nuzzling her cheek against my chest. If she kept fighting her feelings, I was going to have to force those memories into her mind. I really didn't want to do that.

Holding her tight, I remembered doing the same thing when she'd cry in the middle of the night. "We were inseparable, angel. I know we were just kids, but that's where our connection started. You trusted me then."

"I trust you now," she countered seriously.

"Only because I showed you the truth. But I have to say, I'm glad you haven't fully given yourself to me. It shows your strength. You think before you act, even if there are forces pulling you in other directions. You will make a great leader."

Twisting her body, she glanced down at me, crossing her leg over mine. "Thank you for showing me. I needed it."

The wind blew a strand of hair across her face and I slid it behind her ear. "You're welcome. There's nothing I wouldn't do for you."

"Can I ask another question?" I nodded, waiting for her to continue. "What does Maret look like?"

I narrowed my gaze. "Why do you want to see her?"

"I want to see if it sparks something in my memory."

"You're not planning on paying her a visit are you?" I wasn't about to show her so she could run to the north and confront her.

She laughed, but it was sad. "I have no intentions of seeking her out. I only want to see her."

Closing my eyes, I focused on the memories of the last pack meeting before my family was banished. I was there with my parents and Kade was beside me. Maret was always close by my uncle, and that was where I looked. She had long, raven colored hair, but what really made her stand out were her eyes. One was green, the other brown.

"Did you get a glimpse of her?" I asked, opening my eyes.

She nodded. "I did, but I don't remember her. I was hoping that seeing her would make something click in place." Taking a deep breath, she focused on the water and a small smile spread across her lips. "Do you want to go for a swim, like old times? It might not be a frozen lake, but we can imagine it is." Getting to her feet, she held out her hand, but I jumped up and ran toward the water.

"First one there wins," I yelled over my shoulder.

"Asshole," she thundered, chasing after me.

I loved her laugh, even when we were kids. Before getting to the water, I turned around and grabbed her around the waist, hauling her into the waves. When we surfaced, she slapped me on the arm, but I refused to let her go.

"You cheated!"

Chuckling, I pulled us farther into the water, spreading her legs to straddle me. "I never said I played fair."

With her arms around my neck, she smiled and bit her lip. She rocked her hips against mine and I growled, growing hard in an instant. "I don't either."

The second she kissed me, all bets were off.

TWELVE

BAILEY

"I'm ready, Ryker," I moaned, sucking on his bottom lip.

He groaned. "Fuck, angel, you're killing me."

Glancing around the beach, as much as I wanted to give in to my impulses, having sex out in the open wasn't our best option. "Let's go inside."

He kissed me hard, fingers digging into my hips, before he pulled back. "You'll have to give me a minute."

Holding back my snicker, I detached from him and waited until he calmed down enough to get out of the water. By the time we got up to the beach house, we were covered in sand. Before going inside, he grabbed me by the waist, pulling me into the shower. The water started out cold, cooling my burning skin, but it did nothing to calm the ache between my legs.

Without words, he ripped off my bikini top. Kicking off his shorts, he flipped me around. My hands went up on the wall as he knelt down and slowly pulled my bottoms to mid-thigh. Growling, he kneaded my ass and bit down on a cheek. Standing up, he grabbed hold of his cock and rubbed it between my legs.

"Yes," I moaned as the tip hit my sensitive clit. Pushing my body into him, I shimmied my bottoms off and tightened my legs, making the pressure unbearable for both of us.

Leaning over me, he pinched my nipples and sucked on my neck. "Now. It's going to be now," he demanded.

Tilting my head to the side, I bit my lip and met his heated gaze, letting him know I was ready. He grasped my chin and kissed me before pulling back and thrusting inside. The harder he pumped, the closer I was about to come. Standing up straight, he grabbed my hips and pulled me back into him, making a smacking sound each time we connected. His low, strangled growl didn't help because it turned me on even more. My nipples hit the rough siding as I bounced on him, making me crazy with excitement. I ached to find my release, but I knew he would stop the second I got too close.

Before I could give in, he pulled out of me and turned me around with the biggest grin on his face, his wolf eyes shining through. My eyes were glowing with need and he could see it; he found delight in it. "That's exactly what I wanted to see. Can you see it in mine as well?"

I could and it was intoxicating. "Yes," I growled, "let's finish this."

Lifting me in his arms, we kept our eyes on each other as he slid home. My back rubbed against the wall as he pounded into me. In just a matter of seconds, my release came fast and so did his. He shuddered in my arms, releasing his warmth inside me.

Grinning from ear to ear, I pressed my forehead to his. "That was amazing."

His chest rumbled in satisfaction. "And it's just the beginning."

THIRTEEN

BAILEY
TWO WEEKS LATER

"We can't stay here much longer," Ryker said. Coming up behind me, he put his arms around my waist, pressing his lips to my bare shoulder.

I finished braiding my hair and nodded. "I know. Our wolves are getting restless." Without shifting, it was like being in a cage. They were trapped in our bodies. Being at the beach, there were no secluded places to run. "Have you heard anything new from the alphas in your council?"

"Not yet. I'm taking that as a good sign. I did talk to Cedric this morning while you were sleeping. Everything's good there. However, we need to figure out a new place to go. Any requests?"

There were so many places I wanted to see, but we were limited to where our wolves could roam. "How about the mountains here in North Carolina? We can rent the car for a little while longer and leave in the morning."

He kissed my neck and then turned me around. "We can do that," he murmured, gazing down at my body. "Going for a swim?"

I had my bathing suit on, ready to head outside. "I am. Want to join me? We can christen the pool. We've done it everywhere else, why not there?"

Grinning wide, he squeezed my butt and winked. "As soon as I get back, I'll join you." He let me go and grabbed the car keys off the dresser.

"Where are you going?"

"To the store to get food for dinner. I won't be gone long."

As soon as he left, I locked the door behind him and went out the back door to the pool, setting my book down by the edge. Thankfully, the neighbors weren't close by, so if we wanted to have a little fun in the sun we could. With it being early May, the water was cold for human standards, but it felt warm to me. I was used to the cooler temperatures.

Ten minutes had passed and I wanted to be ready for Ryker's return. I untied my top and slid my bottoms off, throwing them to the side of the pool before getting on the float. My book was just at the edge of the pool so I paddled over and snatched it—a flash of something moving caught my eye in the process. *What the hell?*

"Ryker?" I looked around and there was no one there.

A voice spoke up from behind. "Sorry to disappoint you, B."

Growling, I rolled off into the pool and immediately went on guard. "What in the name of all fucks are you doing here?"

Dressed in a pair of slacks and a polo shirt with his blond hair perfectly coifed, Sebastian picked up my bathing suit and tossed it to me. I threw my now wet book at his head, hoping to wipe the smirk off his face. Unfortunately, he dodged out of its path. "It's good to see you too. I see you and Whitemore have gotten closer."

I put my bathing suit on and stormed out of the pool. The rage inside consumed me, my wolf desperate to kill him. "So help me God, if you try to take me back, I'll rip out your goddamned throat right now."

He held his hands up, taking a step back. "I don't want that, Bailey."

I was so angry my claws extended, my body shaking with the need to shift. "Lies," I shouted, my voice animalistic. "All you've done my entire life is lie to me. I know the truth."

His eyes flashed. "No, you don't. That's why I'm here, to tell you the truth. I've followed you ever since you left Wyoming."

Frozen in place, I remembered the way I felt at the airport. I had sensed another wolf for a brief second. "It was you," I whispered.

He nodded. "I wanted you to know I was there."

"Why can't I sense you?"

Taking a deep breath, he blew it out and stared deep into my eyes. "I'm a royal, Bailey. It's part of our magic. I can choose if I want to be sensed or not."

Everything around me stopped, my whole body numb. Sebastian tried to steady me, but I slapped him, raking my claws down the side of his face. "Don't you dare touch me," I hissed. Blood oozed from his wound, but he stood firm. "You were there when I was in college, weren't you? Why didn't you tell me? Was it to keep Ryker away from me?"

Sighing, he wiped the blood off his face and his wound started to heal. "No, it was to protect you. That's been my job since the day you were born. If I didn't keep you away from Ryker, there would've been a war. At the time, you weren't ready for that."

My claws grew longer. "Fuck you! Where were you the day my parents wanted to sell me off to Kade like a common whore? They aren't even my real parents!" The shift came closer. My wolf was demanding his blood.

He took a deep breath, his gaze sad. "I wanted to save you, Bailey. The day that fucker came for you, I was apprehended by his wolves. I'm strong, but not that strong. Besides, I'm worth more to you alive than dead. By the time I killed them and got away, you had already left. I haven't been back since."

"Why should I believe you?"

As fast as lightning, he appeared in front of me, gripping my face in his hands. "Because it's the truth. Look into my eyes and tell me what you see." I grabbed his hands, digging my claws into his skin.

"I see a dead wolf if you don't get your fucking hands off her now," Ryker snarled.

Sebastian huffed, his stare never wavering from mine as he slid his hands down my face. "I don't want to hurt her. She needs to know the truth," he claimed.

"Then I suggest you say it quickly and disappear."

"It's not that simple. I need time." He then grabbed my hands, holding them over his heart. Ryker growled his warning; he was about to attack, his body trembling in rage.

"*Stop!*" I yelled through our bond.

Breathing hard, he tensed, ready to strike. "*He betrayed you. He needs to die.*"

"*I need to hear him out. If he's truly betrayed me, I'll kill him myself.*" He reluctantly stepped back, but stayed on guard.

"Do I get to speak, or are you two plotting my demise?" Sebastian asked.

"Yes to both," I replied.

Squeezing my hands, he lowered his gaze. "I know you think I betrayed you, but I would never do that. I swore to your family, your *real* family, that I would protect you."

"And who exactly is that Sebastian? I can't remember anything about them. The people who I thought were my parents stole me from my family. If I ever see them or anyone from the Yukon pack, I will kill them, just like I'll kill you, royal or not."

"That might be kind of hard," he murmured sadly, his expression grim.

Dread settled into the pit of my stomach. "Why is that?"

"I think you know why, Bailey."

Closing my eyes, I pulled my hands away from his and stepped back. "All of them or just my parents?"

"They weren't your parents."

"Tell me," I commanded, opening my red, burning eyes.

He glanced quickly over at Ryker and then back to me, his expression torn. "I'm not sure. I didn't stick around to find out, but the Yukon's weren't happy. We all know what they're like."

Slapping a hand over my mouth, I held in my scream. Ryker approached, but I held up my other hand. They both looked at me like I was a bomb about to explode. By the ache in my chest, I felt like one. I had to get away.

"Bailey, don't," Ryker pleaded.

Tears fell down my cheeks. I couldn't stay there any longer.

FOURTEEN

RYKER

"Bailey!" Sebastian shouted.

I wanted to chase after her, but she needed to be alone. It killed me to see her in pain. Sebastian started to take off after her, but I stepped in his way. "Let her go."

He glared at me. "She needs to know the rest."

"And she will. Right now, she wants to be alone. She just found out that her pack was most likely slaughtered."

"Fuck them! They weren't her pack. She was their goddamned prisoner; a pawn in their plot to be united with your psycho, piece of shit brother," he thundered.

"But you allowed that to happen, didn't you? You stood by for fifteen years, watching her—*letting* her—be used."

Jaw tense, he huffed and his eyes tracked Bailey's movement toward the water. "I never wanted her to get hurt. I did what I did to keep her safe. Joining the Northern pack was the only way to be with her. I made an oath to her father before he died. He told me to protect her."

"What happened to them?"

He tore his gaze away from Bailey and looked at me. "Greed. I'm not sure of your knowledge about the royals, but we've always been more powerful than the rest."

"Are all royals related?" He shook his head, but kept his focus on Bailey. The way he looked at her, I could tell there was something there. "Are you in love with her?"

He chuckled, but it didn't sound humorous. "Even if I was, it wouldn't matter. You're her mate. That's why you were banished from your pack. Rollin made sure of that."

"My uncle? How do you know all of this?"

"Because I was there, watching from a distance. You had Bailey, but I couldn't get to her with that damn witch of yours casting her voodoo shit everywhere. Your mother had seen the mating signs between you two and went to the council. Unfortunately, Rollin had staked his claim to Bailey first, promising her to Kade. Your parents fought it. Your father even challenged Rollin for his position as alpha."

"But he never got the chance," I said.

"No, he didn't. From what I could tell, he would've won the fight. I don't understand why your father wasn't alpha to begin with."

"He didn't want to kill his brother."

I remembered the morning of the duel, as if it was burned in my brain. My father sat at the kitchen table with his morning coffee, only to fall over dead. It was soon discovered there was wolfsbane in his drink, masked by magic. It was Maret who killed him for my uncle. If either were still alive, I was going to make sure my face was the last they ever saw.

"But given the chance, you would've killed Kade?" he questioned.

"In a heartbeat." Visions of him forcing himself on Bailey flashed in my mind. I would've done more than kill him; I would've tortured him until he begged for death.

"Sometimes I wonder what would've happened if your father was alpha. The attack on my pack probably would've never happened. After your family was murdered, Rollin sent Bailey off to the Northern pack. Her memories were wiped clean so it didn't matter where she was taken to. She didn't even know me when I joined them."

"How did she escape and end up lost in the woods?"

Releasing a heavy sigh, he lowered his head. "When your uncle led the attack, no one knew they were coming. Maret used a masking spell to catch us off guard. By the time we realized what was going on, it was too late. Marrock and Tala, Bailey's parents, stayed and fought 'til the end. Bailey disappeared into the woods, lost with no memories. I tried to catch up to her . . . but you found her first, taking her straight back to the people hunting her."

Eyes wide, I stood there in shock. Her life was a clusterfuck because of me. "You have got to be shitting me," I grumbled. Out in the distance, Bailey sat down on the sand and stared at the horizon. Her feelings weren't all over the place, which was good, but I could still feel the pain of her loss. Even though the Whitehill's weren't her parents, she still mourned them. I felt like complete and utter dog shit. "Basically what you're trying to say is, if I wouldn't have found her, none of this would've happened."

"Who knows at this point?" he answered honestly. "Maybe she might've been killed. I don't know if I would've found her in time. Either way, we can't change the past. What's done is done."

"And she's paid the consequences."

He nodded. "That she has."

I could feel her in my mind, listening to my thoughts. She knew everything. I just hoped she wouldn't blame me for fucking up her life.

FIFTEEN

BAILEY

Ryker sat down beside me in the sand, trying his best to smile. "When you were in college, you always braided your hair and played with it while you studied, just like you're doing now. I thought it was cute."

I laid my head on his shoulder. "Nervous habit. What else did you discover while stalking me?"

He chuckled and put his arm around me. "Your favorite color is green and I'm only saying that because you wore a lot of it. You're smart, kind, generous, and you love to laugh. It took all I had not to go after you, especially when you drew the attention of human men."

I snorted. "They never stuck around long." When I looked up at him, he bit his lip, looking sheepish. "And now I can see why."

He shrugged. "What can I say? I didn't want them touching you. You're mine."

Shaking my head, I kissed his chin. "I am, and just so you know, I don't blame you for anything that happened. I know you feel guilty." It broke my heart listening to his inner turmoil.

"How can I not?"

"You didn't know what was going on when you found me in the woods."

"It still doesn't change the way I feel."

Taking his hand, I held it to my cheek and breathed him in. "That's only one side of the coin. We both lost the ones we loved. If you wouldn't have found me, maybe your family would still be alive. We can either share the guilt, or let it go."

He held me tight. "You are wise beyond your years."

We sat there for a few minutes in silence until Sebastian approached, his energy stronger than before. At least he wasn't trying to hide his presence.

"Bailey," he called out.

Ryker sighed and whispered in my ear. "I don't like the guy, but you might want to listen to what he has to say."

I glanced back at Sebastian. "What if I don't like what I hear?"

"Then kill him." He shrugged and got to his feet. Slapping a hand on Sebastian's shoulder, he spoke low. "Try anything stupid, and I'll snap your neck."

"I'm sure she'll beat you to it," he answered back. Ryker moved out of the way, but stayed close. Sebastian sat down and grabbed a handful of sand, letting it slide through his fingers. "You know you're a royal, but do you really know what it means?"

"No."

"History says that when the first wolves were born, some were touched by the Great Luna and some were not. Over the generations, their bloodlines spread. There are royals everywhere, but a few are more powerful than others. Your family and mine happen to be one of those few."

I gave his words a moment to sink in. "Let me guess, the Northern pack weren't royals."

He scoffed. "Definitely not. That's why they wanted you. They were jealous of your family and wanted the magic for themselves."

"And would it have worked?"

"I'm not sure. But I do know if you and Kade had mated and had kids, your magic would've passed on to them. Imagine a future with Kade's cruelty and your power. It wouldn't have been good."

Ryker's anger blasted through my mind. I glanced over at him with his hands fisted in the sand. Sebastian followed my gaze.

"If you hadn't gotten away from Kade, I was going to kill the fucker myself. I would've gladly sacrificed myself to keep you from that shit show." He turned back to me and I could see the truth in his eyes.

"Then why did you take me back? When you came to get me from school, we could've run away."

"Would you have gone with me?"

"I don't know. Probably, if you could've shown me proof."

He lowered his head, the regret pouring off of him in waves. "There were many things I wish I would've done differently." Taking a deep breath, he lifted his head and watched the waves crash along the beach.

"Why don't I remember seeing Ryker that day?"

"Maret had put a spell on your bond, masking its presence from you. The spell could only be broken once you touched—no magic or spell is strong enough to conceal the power of a mate's bond."

I shook my head. "Why didn't you let me go to him then?"

He looked back at Ryker and then to me. "I couldn't trust him. I hadn't seen him in years and he was Kade's brother. I knew little about the alpha he'd become. I wasn't going to take the chance with your life. You're too important."

We all sat in silence, listening to the waves hit the shore. I could feel Ryker's acceptance of Sebastian's reasoning. *He may even be coming around to the idea of my best friend.* Ryker let out a low growl and I smiled.

"This isn't the first time you've seen the ocean," Sebastian said. "You just don't remember it."

Eyes wide, I gasped. "What?"

He nodded, staring at me with his crystal blue eyes. "You were four years old. I remember making sand castles together." Reaching into his back pocket, he pulled out a wallet and something else. When he held it out to me, my heart stopped. "This is your family, B. Your real family."

In my hands was a picture of a man and a woman with three kids, two girls and a boy. "Oh my God. How do you have this?"

"Your mother gave it to me the night of the attack. She knew what Maret had done to you, how she took your memories, along with those of your brother and sister." He pointed to the two other children in the photo.

My eyes burned and my heart ached. I didn't *want* to know what happened to them, but I needed to. My sister looked like me and our mother, except her platinum blonde hair was wavy and ours was perfectly straight. My brother, however, was the exact image of my father with darker blond hair and striking blue eyes.

"Are they all dead?"

He swallowed hard. "Your parents are. They stayed and fought so we could get away. Your mother made me promise to keep you safe."

"What about them?" I cried, pointing to my siblings.

"They had other protectors, Bailey. I was assigned to you. But if there's one thing I know for certain, I have no doubt they're still alive. I just don't know where they are."

"How do you know that?"

He looked down at the picture. "Because, they were protected by my brothers. They would do anything to keep them safe."

Closing my eyes, I tried to remember them but I couldn't. "I don't even know their names."

"You will," he promised, taking my hand. "We'll get your memories back. Until then, I'll tell you anything you want. Your father," he said, pointing to him in the picture, "was a doctor. His name was Marrock Storm. That's who you truly are . . . a Storm." He gave my hand a little squeeze and continued. "Your mother's name was Tala. She was a Biology professor before you and your siblings came along. After that, she stayed home. You and your brother used to fight all the time."

The thought made me laugh. "What is his name?"

"Colin. Your sister is Faith."

"How can we find them? If your brothers are their protectors, surely you know of a way."

He sighed. "There are ways, but now isn't the time. The Yukon pack is searching for both of us. They are all in at this point; they aren't going to stop."

"What should we do?"

He got to his feet and helped me up. Ryker joined us, his face a mask of uncertainty. Sebastian glanced at him and then back to me. "Whatever we do, we need to stay together. That is, if you'll let me. You're all I have left of our pack."

Our pack. I would give anything to see my family again.

"The choice is yours, angel. If you believe in him, so will I . . . to some extent."

With a small smile, I glanced up at him. *"You sure?"* He nodded and that was all the assurance I needed. "All right," I said to Sebastian, "you're coming with us."

SIXTEEN

BAILEY
SIX DAYS LATER

It felt good to roam free in the woods. My wolf was happy. We'd just gotten back from our daily run and Sebastian was up ahead at the cabin, waiting on Ryker and me to get back. Side by side, we approached in wolf form and watched as Sebastian turned. He was huge and white, just like Ryker. Over the past week, I'd enjoyed hearing Sebastian's stories of my family. I thought for sure we'd have heard something from the other alphas, but there was nothing yet.

Sebastian stalked toward us and then took off into the woods. Ryker had already made it clear he didn't want him encroaching on our time together. And, as long as he respected our space, he was willing to let him stay with us.

Following him up the steps, we shifted back. "The full moon is tomorrow," Ryker claimed. His eyes flashed when I looked at him.

"Your point being . . . what?" I asked with a laugh.

He pulled me into his arms and nipped my neck with his teeth, his erection pushing into my side. "I think you can feel my point."

"I can, but I want to hear it come from your mouth. What do you want to happen on the full moon?"

He cupped my breast and rolled my nipple between his fingers. "I want you to be mine. I don't want to wait any longer." Brushing his lips over my breast, he flicked my nipple with his tongue and I moaned, pushing my breasts out further. A deep chuckle rumbled in his chest. "Is that a yes?"

I didn't have to think twice. "Yes," I breathed.

Picking me up in his arms, he carried me inside and upstairs to our room. Setting me down, he locked the door and stalked toward me. I wasn't about to let him have all the fun. Pushing him against the wall, I kissed him hard and made my way down to his chest. He sucked in a breath when I got on my knees and licked from his abs to the tip of his cock. Grabbing his length, I pumped him while I sucked the tip, smiling as his body jerked in response.

Breathing hard, he groaned and leaned against the wall as I slowly fucked him with my mouth. "Holy shit, angel. I'm going to come if you don't stop."

Wanting a different end result, I sat back on my heels and stared at him. It was his move. Picking me up in his arms, he slammed me down on the bed. He lifted my legs and wrapped them around his head, breathing me in. "Now it's my turn to get a taste of you."

Not wasting any time, he dove in and fucked me with his tongue. I screamed when he sucked on my clit. He chuckled at my response and the vibration of it almost set me off, but he licked me one more time and then slammed into me. I cried out and wrapped my legs around his waist as he made love to me. I didn't want him to stop.

"I'm so close, Ryker."

"Keep going, baby. I want you to scream my name when I come inside you."

Those words were all it took to drive me insane. Screaming out his name, I dug my nails in his back as my orgasm exploded throughout my entire body. Breathing hard, Ryker collapsed on my chest and grunted as he filled me with his release. I loved the feel of him inside me.

"I have to say, that was the best orgasm I've ever had," I admitted breathlessly.

Ryker bit his lip and smirked. "There'll be plenty more where that came from."

About that time, we could hear Sebastian approaching. "Perfect timing."

He laughed and threw on a pair of jeans. "I'll meet you downstairs. Want me to pour you a glass of wine?"

"Sure. I'm just going to take a quick shower first."

Smiling, he opened the door and shut it behind him. It didn't take me long before I was showered and dressed. Sebastian was already sitting at the kitchen bar with a beer when I came down. My glass of wine was right beside him.

"Have a good run?" I asked, taking the seat beside him. Ryker winked at me but then hurried away when his phone started to ring from our room above.

Sebastian took a long gulp of his beer. "It was okay, but would have been better if I couldn't still hear you two from over a mile away."

The blood rushed to my face and I focused on my wine. "Sorry about that."

"Eh, don't worry about it. I know firsthand what it's like to be an unmated male. The need can get a little overwhelming at times."

"Do you think you'll ever find a mate?"

He finished his beer. "I'm sure I will one day. Especially

once you and Ryker complete the bond. You won't need my protection after that."

"Will you be staying with our pack?"

"Do you want me to?"

Nodding, I placed my hand over his. "I do. You're a part of my family. And soon, we're going to find our siblings. We need to reunite the royal pack."

He squeezed my hand. "We will."

Out of nowhere, a blast of anger spiked through my bond. I grabbed my chest and gasped, hoping I could see into Ryker's mind. When I tried, all I could see was red.

Sebastian grabbed me by the shoulders. "Bailey, what's wrong?"

I looked up at the ceiling where Ryker stood just above. "I don't know, but it's not good."

SEVENTEEN

RYKER

"What do you mean 'they took Kami'?" I shouted.

"They came in the middle of the fucking night and took her out of her apartment. They're not giving her back until they find Bailey. They're getting desperate, Ryker." Tate Grayson was one of the toughest alphas I knew, and if he feared for his sister's life it was bad.

"How long have they had her?"

"About eight hours now. They left a note."

"What does it say?"

I could hear the crunch of paper as he gripped it in his hand. "They're going to send pieces of her body back for each day they don't have Bailey, but not until after they've had their fun with her."

"Goddammit!" I yelled. Kami was only eighteen years old and a sweet girl. The thought of them raping and torturing her enraged the fuck out of me.

Bailey and Sebastian appeared at the door, concern etched on their faces. Once my mind cleared, she was able to hear what was going on. *"They want you, Bailey. If we don't go, they'll kill an innocent girl. But if we do . . . I put your life in danger."*

She walked up to me, placing her hands on my face. "Then we go. We have to save her."

With desperation in his voice, Tate replied, "These wolves are out for blood. I need you here, brother. I can't do this alone."

"You won't be. We'll be out there first thing." I hung up the phone and threw it on the bed.

"What's going on?" Sebastian demanded.

"The Yukon pack is desperate to find Bailey. They took a girl hostage, threatening to dismember her if they don't get what they want. We're heading back to Wyoming."

He stalked into the room. "And what, hand Bailey over? Do you have any idea what they'll do to her?"

"Not a goddamned thing. I'll kill them all if I have to."

"So will I," Bailey added, glancing at me before settling her focus on him. "I can't let them hurt an innocent girl because of me. You know I'm a good fighter."

"Yeah, because I'm the one who taught you," he grumbled.

"Then it's all the more reason for me to go."

Sighing, he headed for the door. "Fine, let's go. I can't have you fighting without me."

As soon as he was down the stairs, I grabbed Bailey's hand, pulling her to me. "This isn't how I wanted the full moon to go down."

She nodded. "I know, but we have to do this. There will be plenty of full moons."

I kissed her long and hard. "And I'm sure as hell going to make sure of that."

We were almost to Tate's ranch, which was about three hours north of Jackson Hole, Wyoming, where I lived. Everyone was on edge, including Cedric, who was still back in Jackson. "Are you sure you don't want me there?" he asked.

"No, I need you with the pack."

"What if they outnumber you?"

"Then I guess we'll have our work cut out for us."

"Stubborn son of a bitch. Don't get yourself killed," he snapped.

"Don't plan on it. If everything goes the way we want, we'll be fine." I hung up and tossed my phone into the center console. "Okay, we're almost there. We need to come up with a plan."

"If your main objective is to save the girl, we need her scent," Sebastian explained. "I can track her location and then someone can go after her."

"Why can't you track her and find her yourself?" I asked, glaring at him in the mirror.

"Because I'm not leaving Bailey's side."

"Are you always going to be up her ass?" I snapped.

Bailey slapped me on the shoulder. "That's enough. Stop with the pissing contest."

"She's right. You'll be thanking me once the night's done," he grumbled low.

When we got to Tate's ranch, he was outside with five of his wolves. They tensed when Sebastian got out of the car. Tate walked up to me, but stopped cold, focusing on Bailey and Sebastian.

"Where are they?" I asked, referring to the Yukon wolves.

"Some of them are in town, but I still don't know where

they have Kami." He nodded toward Bailey. "Is that your mate?"

I glanced back at Bailey and nodded. "That's Bailey Storm and her protector, Sebastian Lyall. They're part of the royal pack."

Eyes wide, he stepped past me and bowed his head while the other wolves watched on with curiosity. "My name's Tate Grayson. It's nice to finally meet you. I didn't know there were any living royals."

Sebastian snorted. "That's because we don't pronounce it to the world. I've seen what happens when we do."

Tate turned around, eyes wild. "You need to get the fuck out of here. If I'd known she was a royal, I never would've asked you to come. We can't risk her. If they find out what she is, they'll come after your pack next."

"Not if we kill them first. Besides, they already know what she is. They knew when they stole her the first time."

He threw his hands in the air. "Fuck me. What are we going to do?"

Bailey stepped forward, meeting each of their stares. "*You* aren't going to do anything. Kami's gone because of me. I'm going to make sure we get her back. First, we need to track her. Can someone produce something of hers?"

"I have one of her jackets inside. Come with me," Tate insisted. We all followed him into the house and he brought me a thin, denim jacket. I breathed in her scent and so did Bailey and Sebastian.

Sebastian closed his eyes, clutching the jacket in his hands. "I've got a trail. When do we go?"

Bailey started for the door. "Now. We can't waste any more time. If those cocksuckers said they'll fuck with her, they will. I'm not taking any chances."

I grabbed her arm before she could get outside. "I don't think this is a good idea."

"I agree," Sebastian cut in.

Tate joined us. "I'll have my men go after her. Just point us in the right direction."

Eyes wide, Bailey scoffed. "Are you kidding me? That's your plan to get Kami out *alive*? Because that's our goal here, to see her walk away from this mess. If you waltz in, those wolves will smell you from a mile away. At least, with me and Sebastian, we can mask our scent along with Ryker's." She opened the door and stepped out. "Now, let's go. I, for one, know what it's like to be tormented by those fuckwads."

Clearing his throat, Tate slapped a hand on my shoulder. "She's a pistol, Whitemore. Remind me never to get on her bad side."

Sebastian snorted. "Tell me about it. She's already threatened to kill me on at least three different occasions; not to mention how many times my balls have been on the line."

He joined Bailey outside, but before I could go, Tate squeezed my shoulder. "I'm sorry, brother."

"For what?"

"For putting your mate in danger. I love my sister. I couldn't let them kill her."

"And I would never expect you to. This is my fight, not yours. Besides, they wouldn't have stopped at just Kami. I know those wolves. I used to be a part of their pack."

"When they see you, it won't be the end. They'll hunt your people down."

The thought of that made my blood boil. "They can try, but as you know, I have some of the fiercest warriors in my pack. We won't stop until they're all dead."

EIGHTEEN

BAILEY

"How far away do you think? Four miles?" I asked, peering at Sebastian. Brows furrowed, he closed his eyes and breathed in.

"Roughly," he replied with a nod.

Ryker put his arm around my waist, grabbing my attention. "Why don't you stay as you are and we'll shift? That way you can help Kami and get her out."

"Good idea," Sebastian agreed.

I couldn't argue with them there. "Okay. Let's do this." I could always shift if I needed to, but they had a point. If I was her, I wouldn't just trust any wolf, especially two, unmated males.

Ryker and Sebastian took off their clothes and left them on Tate's back porch. They shifted into their wolves and we were on our way. We ran through the woods and I could smell Kami's scent as if she was right beside me. I'd never tracked anyone before—never had the reason to. Sebastian took the lead and Ryker stayed by my side. Once Sebastian slowed his pace, I knew we were close.

Crouching down, I crept up beside him and focused on

the camp in the distance. There were three tents and four wolves from what I could tell. "She's in one of those tents," I whispered. Sebastian nodded in agreement and padded off slowly.

Ryker nudged me with his nose. *"Stay out of sight during the fight. When all is clear, get Kami out of there. Shift if you have to."*

Grabbing a handful of his hair, I leaned into him. "I will. Be careful."

Without wasting any time, he took off with Sebastian, their howls piercingly loud. Ryker killed one of the wolves instantly while he was still in human form, but the other three had already shifted. Masking my scent, I crept along the camp edge to the first tent. Kami wasn't in there, she was at the far tent, but I had to get past the fighting wolves first.

Ryker attacked first and the fighting began. Their teeth ripped at each other and the smell of blood filled the air. As much as I wanted to fight, I had a job to do. However, blood wasn't the only scent in the air. I finally reached the tent and rushed inside, only to find Kami gagged and bound, surrounded by wolfsbane. Her head jerked in my direction, tears falling down her cheeks.

Holding my breath, I rushed over and untied her, careful not to touch the plants. Grabbing her arm, I wrapped it over my shoulder and lifted her up. Her brown hair was knotted and dirty, her body covered in bruises and fucking bite marks. I growled low, wishing I could rip every single testicle off the dirtbags who did it to her. Quickly, I carried her outside and we both sucked in a huge breath of air.

"Thank you," she gasped, "I thought I was going to die in there."

"We need to get out of here. Can you shift?"

Her face contorted in pain when she moved. "Not yet. Once my adrenaline pumps up, I should be able to." I could only pray that came soon. The fight was still going on, but I had to trust that Ryker and Sebastian would come out on top. Usually we could heal pretty quickly, but Kami was so weak, her body couldn't catch up. We were almost a mile away from the fight when I got the whiff of something foul—another Yukon wolf.

"Fuck me," I hissed.

"I'd be glad to," a voice spoke up from behind.

Kami tensed in my arms, but I squeezed her hand and slid out from under her arm. Whispering as low as I could, I said, "I want you to get away from here as fast as you can."

"She's not going anywhere and neither are you. Now I have two wolf whores to fuck." Anger boiled through my veins and I didn't even bother masking my power. He was going to know who I was, but I didn't care. I turned around and his eyes went wide. "Well, I'll be damned."

I recognized him from the day Kade came to get me. His name was Ansel, one of his friends. I shifted into my wolf and went on the attack, but he was faster than anticipated and ducked. He was bigger than me, yet I was stronger. We circled each other and I lunged, snapping at his neck; he knocked me away, right as I took a bite out of his backside. He growled and nipped my shoulder, but I tore away before he could lock down. Kami was by the trees, trying to shift. I could see the fight in her glowing gray eyes. She wanted revenge.

Ansel attacked and knocked me on the ground, the breath whooshing out of my lungs. He bit down on my shoulder and I howled, the pain radiating through every nerve in my body. I raked my claws over his face, blinding him for only a few seconds so I could get out from under him. He fell over, and then a beautiful gray wolf landed on top of him and attacked. Kami latched onto his throat and jerked as hard as she could. His blood sprayed across the ground and his eyes lost their glow.

Kami huffed and turned her back on him. Before we could take off toward the ranch, Ryker and Sebastian joined us, both smelling of the enemies' blood. Ryker found the wound on my shoulder and growled, but it was already starting to heal. We needed to get out of there before more wolves showed up.

Tate's wolves were all congregated in the back of his house. When they saw us, they grabbed a blanket and raced out to Kami, who collapsed onto the ground. She immediately shifted back and Tate picked her up in his arms, covering her with the blanket.

"What the fuck did they do to you?" he thundered.

"I'll be fine." Then she looked down at me. "Follow us inside. I'll get you some clothes to wear."

I was thankful, considering I ruined mine when I shifted with them on.

Ryker and Sebastian both turned and fetched their clothes from the back porch. I padded past them into the house and followed Tate and Kami into one of the back rooms. "Are you sure you're okay?" he asked her.

She clutched the blanket closer. "Yes. I just need some time." When he left, she opened the closet and pulled out an old high school T-shirt and a pair of shorts. I shifted and put them on. "I'm sorry it's not much, but this used to be my room before I moved out on my own. The only thing left in my closet are things I wore in high school."

I looked down at them and smiled. "No worries. I'm not picky."

"I didn't know you were a royal. I couldn't tell right away when you came to save me. I already know Ryker, but the other wolf, he's a royal too, isn't he?"

"Sebastian? Yes. We can hide our essence from other wolves. It works well if you want to sneak up on someone."

"It feels like I learn something new every day. I don't know if I should bow or curtsy."

"Neither," I exclaimed, holding my hands up, "I'm a wolf just like you."

"With a lot more power and royal blood," she added.

"I didn't know I was a royal until a couple of weeks ago, when I found out my parents were murdered. I didn't have a fairytale life."

She nodded, her expression sad. "I can see that. You must be the one they're after. I heard them talking about you, how they were going to take you up north."

I snorted. "They can try, but I'm not going anywhere. Right now, my concern is for you. What did they do to you?"

Sighing, she averted her gaze. "Things I don't want my brother knowing. He trained me to be a fighter, but I let him down. I couldn't fight against them."

"That's not your fault, Kami. There were four of them and one of you. *They* were the cowards. They were the ones who had to use wolfsbane against you. You're a survivor."

Tears fell down her cheeks. "But they touched me, humiliated me. Their bite marks are all over my skin."

I put my arm around her. "They will heal. The dipshits who did this to you are dead." I paused for a moment. "Did they . . . rape you?"

She glanced up at me. "No, they didn't. With it being so close to the full moon, none of them wanted to chance it. I can't imagine being mated to one of them."

"But you're not of age. The magic of the moon wouldn't have worked."

"That's why I told them I was twenty-three." She smirked.

"Smart girl. I was almost forced to mate with their pack leader. I don't know what I would've done if that had happened."

A knock sounded on the door and Ryker's voice echoed from the other side. "Bailey, can you come out here for a minute?"

"I'll be right there." I squeezed Kami's shoulder and stood. "You sure you're gonna be okay?"

She nodded her head, determination in her gaze. "Of course I'll pull through. I'm more amazed than anything. You came out here and risked your life to save me. I'm worth nothing compared to you, and I am grateful."

"Every life is important and worth just as much as the other. What kind of person would I be if I didn't clean up after my own mess? Your life was in danger because of me and I sure as hell wasn't going to leave you to the wolves."

"What are you going to do to the others tonight when they come?"

"After what they did to you, there's only one thing we can do. Kill them."

NIGHT HAD COME and I was ready to face the others. Tate had called the Yukon pack and let them know where we were.

"What if this is only the beginning?" I asked.

Ryker sighed, his focus on the woods beyond. "Then

we'll keep fighting. You're my mate and I will protect you until my last breath."

The back door opened and Sebastian sauntered out. "That's good. It takes the pressure off of my job."

"No one said you had to keep protecting her," Ryker challenged.

"No, but I'll stay by her side until she tells me to leave." He took the seat beside me and lifted my sleeve. "Wow, you're already healed. That's amazing."

I looked at him and smiled. "The joys of finding your mate."

He rolled his shoulder and hissed. "Maybe I should find mine. My shoulder would feel a lot better if I did."

"You don't have to be my protector anymore, Sebastian. I release you of those duties. You've spent your whole life protecting me. It's time you went out and did something on your own. Maybe even find your mate."

"You could try a dating site," Ryker teased.

Smirking, Sebastian leaned forward. "I'm pretty sure I've gotten more play than you, my friend. I don't need any help. Besides, I kind of like giving you a hard time. I think I'll stick around for a while. That is, if you'll still have me?" he asked, turning to me and grinning wide.

Rolling my eyes, I sat back in my chair. "Is it always going to be like this with you two?"

"Worse if I didn't have you," Ryker replied. "Two unmated, alpha males constantly together isn't a good thing for anyone."

I glanced over at Sebastian who smiled, blinking innocently. "Still want me to join your pack?" he asked.

"I don't know. I'm probably going to have to rethink my decision." I elbowed him in the arm and smiled. It didn't last long because coming from the west side of the woods, a group of wolves approached.

Tate came outside, his body tense, eyes focused on the land. "It's time."

Everyone started for the woods, but Ryker stood back and took my hand. "When the fighting starts, stay as far back as you can. They'll be gunning for you."

"I know. I'll be okay, I promise." We caught up with the other wolves just in time to see the Yukon pack filing in. There were twelve of them and only eight of us. "We're outnumbered."

Ryker leaned in to me. "Yeah, but we have four alphas. We can beat them."

We could, but not without casualties.

"Where is she?" a voice demanded. Immediately, I recognized his voice and gasped. Sebastian glanced back at me, his expression torn. It wasn't just any wolf, it was Darius Whitehill, the father I had known for most of my life. What the hell was he doing leading the Yukon wolves? "Come forward, Bailey. It's time to go home."

Ryker tried to hold me back, but I pushed through, my body shaking with rage. "I will not go anywhere with you ever again."

His gaze found Ryker's and he snarled. "And now I see why. You chose the wrong brother," his focus landed on Sebastian, "and also a traitor. This doesn't look good at all, Bailey. You sure did leave a mess for me to clean up. I almost didn't get out of it with my life."

Ryker and Sebastian moved to the front of the group. "The only mess that'll be left will be your rotten corpses. I'll make sure to send your head to my uncle," Ryker growled.

Darius grinned, his fangs growing longer. "We'll see about

that." Then to his men, he nodded toward us. "Kill the traitor, but leave the young alpha to me. I want my daughter to watch me rip off his head. Maybe then she'll learn obedience."

After that, everything moved in slow motion. The men shifted, except for Darius, who watched on in amusement. The Yukon wolves gunned for Ryker and Sebastian. Howls filled the air, along with the smell of death. I couldn't tell who had fallen or which side everyone was fighting for. There was one howl that rose above the rest. My heart shattered as I watched Sebastian fall to the ground with a fatal wound to his belly. His eyes found mine and I screamed out his name.

There was another wolf about to finish him off, but I grabbed a tree limb off the ground and threw it like a spear, piercing it through his gut. Ryker ran over and ripped out his throat. Darius' laugh could be heard echoing through the trees. Sebastian growled low, but he couldn't get up. Wrapping my arms around his neck, I tried to lift him, but he was too heavy.

"Dammit, Sebastian, don't you dare die on me. You hear me?" More howls filled the night, more death. Tears ran down my cheeks, but I wasn't about to give up on him. I had to get him away from the fight. Grabbing his legs, I pulled him as far as I could until an arm grabbed me around the waist.

"It sure is good to see you again, *darling*," Darius whispered into my ear. "I've missed you." He jerked me away from Sebastian, holding me tight around the neck.

"You're a lying son of a bitch," I hissed, digging my claws into his arms. "Let me go." His hold was so tight, I could barely breathe. Then, he injected something into my neck and my claws retracted.

I tried to shift, but nothing came. "What the hell did you give me?"

He chuckled. "Don't worry, it's not enough to kill you. Just a subtle dose of wolfsbane mixed with a sedative." Panic consumed me, especially when I could feel the serum burning like acid in my veins. "Be a good girl and stop kicking. I thought I raised you with better manners."

I got one last look at Ryker fighting off the wolves and Sebastian lying still on the ground before he hauled me over his shoulders. *"Ryker . . ."*

Darius only had time to take two more steps until the loudest growl I'd ever heard echoed through the air. He dropped me to the ground like a sack of potatoes, and I hissed in pain.

Out of the twelve Yukon wolves, only two were barely still alive. We were faring better, but still had one dead and two injured. Sebastian was nowhere to be found. *"Where's Sebastian?"*

Ryker responded, his voice tense. *"I don't know."*

My head felt fuzzy and my vision started to blur. Darius stood his ground and clapped, but blocked me from Ryker's sight. "Well done, my friends. You're a lot stronger than I gave you credit for." He was too confident, especially with being outnumbered.

"Ryker . . . h—he's up to something."

"What the fuck did he do to you?"

The edges of my vision turned dark. I was about to lose consciousness. *"Poison."*

Darius slowly reached behind his back and pulled two liquid vials from his pocket. Even though my vision was blurry, I could still see the blue petals of wolfsbane inside. His muscles tensed and I knew what he was about to do.

"No!" I screamed. Grabbing the first thing I could find, I grasped the tree limb and hurled it right at Darius, at the man I thought was my father. It pierced him in his belly and the sound of him choking on his blood made my stomach curl. Falling to his knees, he looked down at the limb and then over to me. The darkness crept in, but I was able to watch as Sebastian came from out of nowhere, baring his fangs. The last thing I saw was him ripping Darius' head off and watching it roll onto the ground. I went under with a smile on my face.

Sebastian was alive and the enemy was dead.

NINETEEN

RYKER

THREE DAYS LATER

I poured myself a cup of coffee, and watched Sebastian gulp his down as if it wasn't steaming hot.

"When do you think she'll wake up?"

I shrugged. "I don't know." Seraphina had said there was only a small amount of wolfsbane in her injection, just enough to keep her capacitated for a few days. We'd just have to wait for her body to flush it out.

"Do you think she'll be pissed at me?"

"For what, pretending you were about to die?" He nodded. "I don't know. From one alpha to another, it was brilliant. But she was terrified when she watched you go down. I didn't realize she liked you that much."

"Jealous?"

"Hardly," I answered with a smile.

As much as the guy got on my nerves, his only concern had been for Bailey. I couldn't fault him for that. After setting his cup in the sink, he walked to the door and took off his shirt. "I'm going for a run."

Tyla showed up as he was making his way out the door.

She was carrying a large paper bag in her hands, and watched him exit.

"*Please* tell me you're not interested in that douchebag."

She snorted. "As if. I totally have better taste than that." She said it but I didn't believe it. "I guess she's still not awake?"

Sighing, I moved over to the couch. "No." She sat beside me and set the paper bag on the coffee table. "What's in there?"

Grinning wide, she pulled out the contents. "My mother made you some soup and I brought two loaves of my homemade bread and chocolate chip cookies. Bailey hasn't eaten in three days. I'm sure she'll be starving when she wakes up."

"Thanks. She'll love it."

"I guess your plans to mate on the full moon were thwarted. You'll have to wait three more weeks now."

"True, but it's not that big of a deal." She nodded, but I could tell she was keeping something from me by the smile on her face. "What is it?"

She bit her lip. "Okay, so I don't know if you've talked to Bailey about this, but I wanted to do something special for her. Ever since she's been here, we've become pretty close. Anyway, I know she's always wanted a wedding, but it's not something we do. Maybe on the next full moon, we could throw a party?"

"Like what exactly?"

"I don't know, maybe a reception of sorts, like they do at human weddings. I think Bailey will like it. After everything that's happened, it'll be something to get our spirits up. Besides, I think it's time our pack makes its own traditions."

I could hear Bailey stirring in the room above. Her mind

was in turmoil over the death and betrayal of the only father she'd ever known. His face ran through her mind and I could feel her pain. "I think you might be right." Her eyes lit up. "But let's make it a surprise. I'll leave the details to you."

She squealed, getting to her feet. "I'm on it. Kami and I have already been talking details."

"You already planned this before I gave consent?"

She rushed to the front door and winked. "I knew you would say yes. You'd do anything for her."

"Yes, I would." She walked out the door and then shortly after, the sound of Bailey's footsteps thumped on the hardwood floor.

Stopping at the top of the stairs, the sound of her growling stomach could be heard from where I sat, even without my sensitive wolf hearing. "Do I smell cookies?"

I opened the bag and pulled them out; they were still warm. "Freshly baked from Tyla's kitchen. You better hurry before I eat them all."

Jumping down the stairs, she rushed over and snatched the one out of my hand and closed her eyes, moaning as she bit into it. "Holy hell in a handbasket. These taste so good."

"She made you some soup too. I have to say, she's doing a better job than I am. The last thing I thought about was food. I just wanted you to wake up." I gave her the bowl of soup and she devoured it.

"Well, I'm back now. Whatever that shit Darius gave me, it's not something to play around with. My blood still burns, but not as bad as before. If the Yukon pack starts using wolfsbane against their enemies, we might have a problem."

I nodded. "I know. It just shows us what cowards they really are. They can't beat us in a normal fight, so they resort to other methods. Nevertheless, I don't want to imagine what would've happened if Darius had thrown one of those vials at me. Thanks to you, I didn't have to find out." After examining the vials, there was a lethal dose of wolfsbane in them. I wouldn't have survived if it had exploded on my body.

"How's Sebastian? I was so afraid I'd lost him."

"So you weren't worried about me?" I teased.

She pursed her lips. "*You* didn't get hurt. How is he?"

"He's still around, succeeding brilliantly at being a pain in my ass." She jabbed me in the side and I grabbed her hand and held it. "He's worried about you. He pretended to be fatally injured to psych Darius out. When you freaked out, it helped make him believe Sebastian's wounds were serious. The only thing he didn't anticipate was you being caught up in the middle."

"So he faked it all? That son of a bitch."

"He did what he had to, Bailey. You believing he was about to die made Darius lower his guard."

"So, tell me the truth. Are you guys getting along yet?"

I chuckled. "We're getting there. But if you want him to be a part of our pack, we have to figure out new living arrangements. Having his alpha ass in my house isn't going to work."

She snickered. "Don't want to share me?"

I pulled her into my lap and kissed her. "Fuck no. I want you all to myself. He can still be your protector, but I can't have him interfering."

She held me tight, with her arms around my neck, rubbing her body against mine. "It can't be all that bad," she moaned.

Then as if on cue, Sebastian opened the front door and I snorted. "Trust me, it *can*."

TWENTY

BAILEY
ONE WEEK LATER

"I know this'll make lover boy happy," Sebastian announced.

Laughing, I helped him unload the last of his furniture into his new house. He was only five minutes down the road. "You're not that far away. Besides, I should've let you move your own shit after what you pulled."

"You're still sore over that?"

"I thought you were dying, jackass!"

"I did it to save you, but in the end, you saved me. I know it couldn't have been easy to kill him." I tried to hide my pain, but failed. "It's okay to be sad, Bailey. Darius was your father for most of your life. Even I didn't know all of his plans until much later. I wish I could've gotten you out sooner, but I had to wait until you were ready. And even then, I was too late."

"You were never fast enough to catch me."

"I'm faster. You were just better at hiding." We both laughed and it felt good.

Taking his hands, I looked up into his bright blue eyes.

"I was serious when I relieved you of your duties. You don't have to protect me anymore."

"I know, but old habits die hard. I've been responsible for you for years. It's not easy starting a new life, or finding a new pack."

"You'll get used to it. I don't want you missing out on life because of me. The only thing I need from you is your help in finding our siblings."

Nodding, he sat down on his new leather couch. "It'll take some time, but I can do it. I know my brothers . . . I just need to look in the right places."

I sat down with him. "Do you miss them?"

"I miss a lot of things, B. One day, when you get your memories back, you'll see how amazing pack life can be. Ryker seems to be moving in the right direction. It's strange how much his ways are just like your father's."

The thought made me smile. One day I'd remember my mother and father. Maybe then I wouldn't feel so lost. "Speaking of Ryker, I have to meet him at the ranger station. He's taking me hiking, so I can see what it is he does for a living."

He got up and helped me by taking my hand. "What about what *you* want to do for a living? You're not going to waste your degree are you?"

"No. I'm going to apply to different schools this summer. At least my fake parents did *something* right."

"They had no choice. They knew you'd rebel if you didn't get your way. You're an alpha; you could've easily fought your way out."

I nodded. "I didn't want to hurt anyone, at least, not until Kade. Do you think Rollin will try to retaliate? I killed Kade and now Darius. He isn't going to like the humiliation if word gets out."

"He may not be happy, but I don't think he's stupid enough to keep trying. He won't have a pack left." He pushed me toward the door. "Now go, before Whitemore comes here looking for you. I'd hate to have to kick his ass."

"I'll have to tell him you said that," I replied with a wink. He opened the door and I got in Ryker's Jeep. I had gotten my license just like a normal person when I turned sixteen, but I was never given a car or allowed to have one. I was enjoying this new freedom immensely.

When I pulled up to the ranger station, Ryker was standing outside with Cedric. "Hey, babe," he greeted, leaning into the car to give me a kiss.

"Hello yourself." Then to Cedric, I smiled. "And to you. Busy day?"

He shrugged. "Same as every day, except we did see a few bears today. They tucked tail and ran when they saw these," he said, flexing his biceps.

Ryker smacked him on the back of the head, laughing. "Keep telling yourself that." He leaned into my window and whispered low. "They snarled and huffed at him before leisurely walking away. Don't let him fool you."

"Thanks for ruining it, Whitemore." He started for his car and opened the door. "What trail are you taking her on?"

Ryker looked at me and smiled. "I was thinking about the Hidden Falls trail, out past Jenny Lake."

"Ah, that's a good one. Probably lots of snow out that way. I don't think anyone's been on it yet. Have fun!" He got in his car and took off out of the parking lot.

Ryker opened the car door and held out his hand. "You ready? We're going to ride in my truck."

Looking up at the thick, gray clouds, I breathed in the cool, crisp air and could already smell the approaching rain.

"More than ready," I said, taking his hand. We got in his truck and started down the road.

"There aren't that many tourists out this way. When do they usually come?" At each trailhead we passed, there were only one or two cars in the parking lots. The snow was abundant on the mountains, but that was what I liked. From what I learned, it stayed on the mountains well into the summer.

"The tourists start rolling in by the end of May and on through the summer, when the mountains are green and the flowers are in bloom. Right now, there's still plenty of snow, and since it's melting, the falls should be amazing." He turned into the Jenny Lake trailhead and parked.

I got out of the truck and couldn't stop from smiling at the way Ryker looked, all professional in his uniform. "I always thought men in uniform were sexy."

Grinning wide, he glanced down at his clothes. "That's what all the ladies say."

"I have no doubt. Do the tourists ever want pictures with you?"

He chuckled. "Sometimes, but it's mostly kids."

"And do you get your picture taken with them?"

"Of course. I like seeing families bring their kids out here and experiencing the excitement in their eyes when they see the mountains. It's hard to find people who appreciate our land as much as we do. That's why I do what I do, just like you chose to be a teacher."

We marched across a small bridge where two human men were fishing. They nodded at us when we passed. The further we went along the trail, the deeper we went into the woods. "What happens if you have a lot of bear activity?"

He picked up a fallen branch and moved it out of the way. "We close the trail down."

"Do people adhere to those warnings?"

"Not all the time. Sometimes the tourists want to have a close encounter so they can get pictures. Then when they do, they panic and end up getting hurt. You can't fix stupid."

We hiked along the trail for about an hour and still no waterfalls. "How far do we have to go?" The farther we went, the more snow there was.

Ryker glanced down at the ground. "Nowhere close. The snow is only a foot deep here. When it reaches four feet, we're almost there."

"Four feet? Wow," I gasped in awe.

We continued on our way and there weren't any trees or limbs blocking the path. The only thing that raised alarm bells was the grizzly feces on various parts of the trail. If I were human, I'd be terrified. We climbed over a bunch of rocks and then found ourselves hidden underneath a blanket of trees. The snow started to get deeper.

"Is that what I think it is?" I pointed to a bridge up ahead that overlooked a small set of waterfalls. However, the water wasn't what got my attention.

Ryker grinned wide. "Yes it is, baby. I told you it'd get up to four feet."

The snow on the bridge was partially melted, but on the other side it was almost like a different land. The snow was higher than the bridge and the fences both. You could see the top posts sticking out of the snow. All it would take was one slip and I'd fall into the rushing water below. Ryker climbed up first and held out his hand.

"I won't let you fall."

I took his hand. "You better not."

He pulled me up onto the hard packed snow. "Be careful where you step. I don't want you getting lost." There were holes in the snow where you could see all the way down to the bottom. A person could easily break their leg if they fell in. The sound of the waterfalls grew louder as we edged closer. Once we got past the trees, I got the most magnificent view of the cascading water.

"I think I'm jealous," I grumbled.

Ryker glanced back at me, brows furrowed. "Why?"

I pointed to the falls. "Because you have all this. I've never seen such beauty."

He grasped my face with his strong hands and kissed me. "You have it now too. There are so many places out here I want to show you. If you want, I can take you to Yellowstone for a couple of days. It's overrun with tourists, but you need to see it at least once."

"Sounds like a date."

His gaze caught something over my shoulder. "Hang tight, there's something in the middle of the trail up ahead. I'll move it and then we can go." I watched him start up the path and move a boulder off to the side, along with a few other rocks that had fallen down the mountain.

While he finished up, I strolled along the snow, leaving a set of my footprints. Then, as if everything clicked into place, I recognized my surroundings. The tree I stood by was the one I hid behind in my last vision. I didn't realize it would happen so soon. Grabbing a handful of snow, I rolled it into a ball and hid.

"Angel, where are you?" Ryker called.

Holding in my snicker, I knew exactly where he'd be. I could see the vision clearly in my mind. Before he could attack, I circled around the tree and hurled the snowball right at his head, hitting him right between the eyes.

He fell to the ground and laughed. "You're gonna regret that."

It was exactly what he'd said in the vision. I stood there, smirking, with my hands on my hips. "Don't think so. I'm not afraid of the big bad wolf."

"We'll see about that." He jumped to his feet and chased after me. All I could do was laugh as he gained on me. I knew what was about to happen and it made my heart race. It wasn't long before he lunged and we went tumbling down to the ground.

With his body on top of mine, he peered down at me, his emerald green eyes raw with passion. "I let you catch me," I told him.

He chuckled. "You would've tired out eventually. We both know I'm stronger."

"Want to put that to the test? I'll fight you, right here and now."

Brushing his thumb across my lips, he leaned closer. "So stubborn. You said the same thing to me when we were kids."

"I know," I murmured.

"You do?"

I nodded. "You told me. We used to play out by the lake and ice skate. Every time I'd fall, you'd laugh. You said it used to piss me off."

His gaze narrowed. "I don't remember telling you that."

"It's because you didn't yet."

"What do you mean, I didn't *yet*?" he asked, searching my face. When I didn't respond, I let him search my mind. He wasn't happy with the outcome.

Holding his face in my hands, I pulled him closer. "The vision doesn't mean anything. Just because it's happening now doesn't mean we don't have a future. Besides, we're already changing it right now." Sighing, he lowered his gaze to my lips. "Tell me about our times at the lake. I want to hear you say it. What happened after I laughed at you?"

"I broke the ice one day, hoping you'd fall through. When it went as planned and you didn't resurface, I got really scared. Screaming your name over and over, I freaked out and jumped in after you. I panicked when I couldn't find you and ended up needing the help myself. You were playing a joke on me the entire time." A sad smile splayed across his lips.

"And I felt like shit when I saw you struggling. From that day on, I made a promise to myself to protect you." I thought about my words. "Do you think that's what happens when wolves realize who their mates are?"

"I don't know, it could be. From what I hear, most mates don't find each other until they're older. Our signs started pretty young. All I knew was, you were special—mine to protect."

My heart thumped hard in my chest. I knew what was about to come. "And what do you know now?" I asked, whispering the words.

Cupping my cheek, he leaned down and kissed me, long and deep. I fisted my hands in his hair and tasted him, putting it all into memory. Whatever happened, I wasn't going to lose any more of my life's memories. He pulled back, ending the kiss too quickly. "I know that I'd give anything to get your memories back. I just want you to remember me."

"I do too. Even if I don't, it's not going to change anything. I know how I feel now."

He tucked a strand of my hair behind my ear, his finger grazing my neck. "And I know how *I* feel. I'll protect you no matter the price, mated or not, even if it costs me my life." His serious green gaze locked into mine. "I love you, angel."

A tear escaped the corner of my eye. I knew he was going to say it, but it was different seeing it in a vision compared to actually experiencing it. "I love you too."

Grinning wide, he wiped away my tear. "Did you see me say that in your vision?"

I nodded. "It was a lot better hearing you say it for real."

Even though he was smiling, I could feel the turmoil inside him. My vision had already come to pass, meaning our future was uncertain. The only thing left to do was take each other's blood and see what was to come.

"You need to stop stressing about the future," I whispered the words across his lips. "At the next full moon, we'll complete the bond and I'll be yours for the rest of our lives. Nothing is going to change that. You can't let some vision be the judge of everything."

He nodded, even though his expression was grim. "I know. I just can't shake the feeling that something's about to get fucked all to hell."

Biting my lip, I took his hand and placed it between my legs. "You got that right. And I think now's the perfect time."

A deep rumble vibrated in his chest. He slipped his fingers inside my underwear and I spread my legs. I gasped when he pushed one inside me and then another.

"I just want you to focus on what's right in front of you. We make our own choices."

He slid my pants down and freed his cock. Sitting up, he pulled me on to his lap. "That we do. Now show me what you want."

Taking him inside me, I moaned as my body stretched around him. "Gladly."

TWENTY-ONE

BAILEY

"And why are we going to the bar again?" I asked.

Tyla checked her makeup in the rearview mirror. "For drinks, why else?" She winked over at me. "Don't worry, I've been sworn to keep all men away from you."

"By Ryker or Sebastian?"

"Both." She giggled.

Groaning, I sat back in the seat. "I swear, they're both going to drive me insane. Although, I never thought I'd see them actually getting along." For the past week, Sebastian stayed close, while Ryker continued with his ranger duties; it was all Ryker's doing. They still gave each other a hard time and were quick to inform me that wasn't going to change.

"That's a good thing though. Having two sexy wolves guarding you is a dream come true. If they weren't both alphas, with one being your mate, you could probably have yourself one hell of a ménage a trois."

I burst out laughing. "Not going to happen with those two. Besides, even if Ryker and I weren't mates, I don't see Sebastian in that way." I shivered and pretended to gag.

She snorted. "You're the only female in the pack who doesn't drool over him. Even I'd love to have a bit of royalty in me for the night." She drove around downtown Jackson Hole until we got to the bar. There were cars everywhere, even more than a usual Friday night.

"What's going on down here? It's never this crowded," I stated.

Luckily, she found a parking space right in front of the bar. It was the only one open in a three block radius. "What do you know . . . a spot right out front. Someone must love us."

We got out of the car and I put on the fitted denim jacket I bought to go over my dress. The night was breezy and cool, exactly how I loved it. Turning my attention to inside the bar, I could tell it was packed, and not with your normal human patrons; there were wolves. A lot of them. I narrowed my gaze and looked at her.

Smiling wide, she took my hand and walked me to the door. When she opened it wide, my mouth hit the floor. Everyone inside stopped what they were doing and regarded me with their attention. Some even cheered and hollered out my name. I didn't know what to do other than give a stupid little wave.

I recognized some, but there were a lot I didn't know. Right in the middle of them all was Ryker, dressed in a plaid button down shirt and jeans, smiling devilishly at me. "What's going on?" I whispered to Tyla.

She waved at someone from across the room and Kami bounced over, dressed in a cute pink dress and cowgirl boots. Hugging me, she said, "You made it just in time!"

"Just in time for what?"

Ryker walked through the crowd toward me and grabbed my hands. "To show everyone you're mine."

Kami snickered and put her arm around Tyla. "We wanted to tell you sooner, but we thought it'd be better as a surprise."

"Surprise?" I looked up into Ryker's mischievous green gaze and searched his mind. Wolves never had weddings like humans, where you exchanged rings. We could never wear them or any kind of jewelry when shifting. The magic of the moon was stronger than any verbal vow or wedding ring.

Smiling, he pulled me close. "We can always have a wedding if you want, but we thought having somewhat of a reception would be similar. Everyone came from all over to meet you."

It was amazing seeing everyone together, laughing and talking without animosity. "I don't need a wedding, Ryker. This is perfect." Squeezing his hand, I nodded toward the crowd. "Let's mingle." There were a ton of faces I didn't recognize but Ryker introduced me to every single one. "I can't believe you know every person here," I whispered in awe.

He chuckled. "I have a good memory."

"All right it's time for me to steal him away," Cedric announced, slapping a hand on Ryker's shoulder.

I put my hands on my hips. "Oh yeah, why is that?"

"Stripper time, why else?" When he saw the expression on my face, he balked and held up his hands. "Holy fuck, Xena Warrior Princess, I was kidding. I'm not stupid enough to have done that; I'd like to keep my balls."

Ryker burst out laughing. "You sure as hell weren't going to have any if you were serious."

"No shit. Good thing I am only taking you to the bar."

Cedric looked back at me, "You don't want to see Whitemore dance without a little bit of liquor in his system."

With a smirk on his face, Ryker pushed him away. "Cocksucker. I dance better than you."

"I never claimed I was good. Now let's go. I think the ladies want to steal your woman away." He nodded toward something behind me and when I turned, Tyla and Kami were there.

Tyla grabbed my hand. "He's right."

Ryker kissed my cheek and nipped my ear before disappearing with Cedric to the bar. All the alphas were there, lifting their shot glasses. *"Don't get into too much trouble over there,"* I sent through our bond.

Lifting his glass, he peered back at me and winked. *"Same goes to you, angel."*

"So what are we going to do if we're not getting drunk with the guys?" I asked the girls.

They giggled and pulled me over to a corner where at least thirty unmated female wolves waited for me, including Seraphina. "They all wanted to ask you questions," Tyla informed me.

I sat down and smiled at all the women. Some were old, but a lot of them were around my age. "All right, let's hear it."

A girl in her mid-twenties from one of the red wolf packs spoke up. Her name was Emma Redding, cousin to the alpha of her pack. She had long, strawberry-blonde hair and green eyes. "How did you know Ryker was your mate?"

The question made me smile. "I didn't at first, but then again, I'm stubborn. You also need to take into account that the people who raised me never told me about *true* mates. Were your parents true mates?"

She nodded, her gaze sad. "My father was killed by a

rogue a couple years back while hunting. My mother doesn't like to talk about him because it pains her. We only have one mated couple in my pack and they're much older. It's hard to get a fresh take on things."

"I understand. Is that how it is with the rest of you? I know Tyla's parents are true mated." I glanced around and they all nodded. "Tell me about your parents, Tyla. What have they said about it?"

All eyes turned her way. "Not much other than it's just a feeling they got. They said I would *know* when it happened."

"And you will," I began, catching their attention, "it's just again . . . I was stubborn. I had to have proof and when I got it, it was still hard to grasp. None of it made sense to me."

"That's because she had her memories taken away by the Yukon pack witch," Kami interrupted.

"She's right, I did. I met Ryker a long time ago when I was just a girl. We were friends and it was because of that close friendship I think our bond was formed. I'd give anything to remember that time with him. Maybe one day, I will. However, I don't think the Great Luna just randomly chooses two wolves to be mates. I think it happens over time when a connection is formed."

"So we don't need to sit on our asses and wait for them to come to us?" Tyla asked.

Everyone laughed and I shook my head. "No, I think you need to get yourselves out there, talk to them. Ryker and I were not born a part of the same pack. Just because your mate isn't with your own pack, doesn't mean he's not out there. Take a look around," I said, waving my hand about. "There are wolves here from all over the country. If you have brothers, cousins, friends, introduce them to some of the women here in this group. I fully believe the magic will come back to our people. You just need to believe in it—have faith."

I could see the determination in their eyes and it brought me joy. The magic of the moon would come back to them; I had no doubt.

"And I think I just found the wolf I'll introduce myself to. He just walked through the door," one of the girls said happily.

I didn't even have to look to know it was Sebastian. He winked at the group of females and marched straight to the bar. The little stinker knew exactly what he was doing. The women all separated and flocked around him and the other men at the bar. There was a strong chance their mates were in that very room.

"Sebastian sure can be a conceited jackass sometimes," Tyla grumbled.

I chuckled. "That he can. He just needs a woman to tame him."

"I'm sure he has a fair share to choose from. Look at them all lining up to talk to him."

He sat at the bar with three females, hanging on his every word. Tyla watched on, her jaw tense and eyes blazing. "If I didn't know any better, I'd say you were jealous," I told her.

She rolled her eyes and turned her back on him. "Don't think so, B. He has a smokin' hot body, but I don't want a wolf who's fucked more women than I can count. I bet he goes home with one of them tonight."

"I doubt that. He may be a ladies man but he's not a douche, well, at least not around me. Have you ever tried to talk to him? Like *really* talk to him?" I inquired.

She huffed. "No. I doubt he'd want anything to do with me."

Grabbing her arm, I squeezed, hissing my words so only she could hear. "Are you even listening to yourself? You are an amazing woman who deserves to find her mate. You said it yourself, you can't wait on them to come to you. Grab the reins and take control."

"Take control of what?" Ryker asked, coming up behind me with his arms around my waist.

Tyla backed away. "And that's my cue to go. Have fun tonight, guys. You both deserve it." She sauntered off quickly and I wasn't surprised to see she didn't head in Sebastian's direction.

Ryker turned me around to face him. "What's up with her?"

"Just girl stuff."

"Then I don't want to know." The music started playing over the speakers and he smiled. "Wanna dance?" Everyone moved away from the floor, giving us our space.

"How can I say no when everyone's watching?" I laughed.

"Exactly." Taking my hand, he led me out onto the floor, wrapping his strong arms around my waist. In that moment, nothing else existed but me and him, and the sound of a country love song. We moved in perfect rhythm with each other, almost like clockwork.

"I didn't think you could dance," I teased.

He winked. "There's not much to it. Besides, we move pretty well together in bed. The dance floor shouldn't be much different."

My cheeks started to burn. "Thank you for this. I think this will be the beginning to something new. Look at everyone. There's bound to be someone coming out of this with a potential true mate." Before the party really got started, there was still some separation amongst the packs, especially between male and female. Territory always played a factor when it came to that. The beta males never approached a female from another pack. I'd wanted those lines to be crossed and now they had.

Ryker glanced around the room, satisfied with the outcome. "I think this is what everyone needed." We danced to the rest of the song and then the next one started; it was upbeat and fast.

Grabbing my waist, he held me against him while I moved my hips to the beat. Everything was perfect until I felt a blast of magic sweep through the room. It was sudden and meant to be quick, like Sebastian had done at the airport. Only, it wasn't him. But it was definitely a royal.

Ryker saw the expression on my face. "What's wrong?"

"Someone's here."

Sebastian left the women at the bar and hurried over. "Did you feel it?" he asked, his gaze concerned.

I grabbed Ryker's hand. "Another royal wants us to know they're outside. Who could it be?"

Sebastian glanced around the room. "I don't know, but I say we go find out."

"Let's go out the back. That way no one will see us leave," Ryker suggested.

We smiled at everyone in passing and disappeared to the back hall. My heart thumped wildly in my chest as I got closer to the door. Sebastian and Ryker went out the door first, both looking in the opposite directions. "No one's here," Ryker grumbled.

I stepped outside. "I know I felt something."

Sebastian marched down the sidewalk. "So did I. Someone's here."

Across the street, standing in a dark corner was a man with whitish blond hair—an Arctic wolf. I had enough time to see his eyes flash before he disappeared into an alley. "Over there," I said, pointing toward a taller building.

Sebastian stepped in front of us. "You guys follow on his trail. I'm going to cut him off on the other side. I'll meet you there."

He took off and Ryker and I rushed across the street. The guy had just turned around another corner, but I could see his moving shadow. He wasn't in a hurry, which made me wonder what the hell he was doing. Why would he walk away when he obviously wanted to be found?

"Why would another royal be here?" Ryker asked.

"I don't know, but we're about to find out." We turned the corner and there he was, leaning against the brick wall. Sebastian crept up behind him, but stopped cold when he got closer.

The rogue wolf raked his gaze over me and chuckled, his body hidden in the shadows. "Look at you, all grown up. It's good to see you again, princess."

Ryker stood protectively beside me. "Who are you?"

The guy stepped out into the light and I gasped. "Holy shit. You look just like—"

"Me," Sebastian answered, approaching cautiously. When he got a good look at the stranger, he smiled and shook his head. "Well, I'll be damned."

TWENTY-TWO

BAILEY

"I knew you'd come out here and find me," the guy said.

Sebastian chuckled and pulled him in for a hug. They looked so much alike, it was uncanny. Sebastian let him go and faced me. "Bailey, this is Micah, my eldest brother." Then he turned to Ryker. "Micah, this is Ryker Whitemore, Bailey's soon to be mate, and alpha of the Teton pack."

"You look like twins," I murmured in awe.

Micah smiled. "We got that all the time. We're actually seventeen months apart, just like you and your sister, Faith."

I gasped. "Where is she? Are you her protector?"

He nodded. "For all of her life. She wanted to come but I didn't think it was safe. We live out by Yosemite."

"Does she remember anything about me or our family?"

"Not at first, but I told her everything. She's on pins and needles back home, waiting to hear if you're who we thought you were."

"What happened the night of the attack? Where did you go?" Sebastian asked.

Micah looked at us all. "When the Yukon pack came, I

took Faith and kept running. Marrock loaded up a duffel bag full of money and told me to get her as far away as I could. We ended up in California and that's where we stayed. When I heard about a royal female showing up in these parts, I had to know who it was. I knew if it was Bailey, you would be by her side."

"Why would you leave Faith by herself?" Ryker cut in. That was a good question.

Micah sighed. "It was either that or bring her here. I heard about the attack from the Yukon pack. The last thing any of us need are two female royals to entice them. I wanted to make sure it was safe before bringing her here."

"I understand," I said.

He glanced back and forth between me and Ryker. "Congratulations on finding each other. Not everyone's so lucky."

Sebastian snorted. "That's a whole other story. Hopefully, Faith hasn't been a pain in the ass like this one," he said, pointing to me.

Ryker chuckled under his breath and I elbowed him in the side. "Hey, I wasn't *that* bad. Try living with a pack you think is your family only to have them turn around and mate you off to a sadistic bastard."

"Who also happened to be Whitemore's brother," Sebastian added. Ryker tensed beside me; it would always be a sore subject for him.

Micah's eyes went wide. "It looks like I have a lot to catch up on."

"That you do," I said, "and you can start tomorrow, when you both leave to get my sister. Right now, we have a party to go to."

Sebastian stared at me, his gaze concerned. "I don't

think it's a good idea for me to leave right now. I want to wait until after the full moon."

I took his hand and squeezed. "I'll be fine. You forget I can take care of myself. Not to mention, I have Ryker. You just saw your brother for the first time in over a decade. Maybe you two can figure out how to find the rest of our pack, including our brothers."

Sebastian wanted to fight me on it, but with Ryker there he backed down. "All right, if you want me to go, I will. I'll help bring your sister back safely."

"That's all I want." I watched them disappear around the corner, as I stayed with Ryker who backed me into the wall.

"I wonder what the packs are going to think when yet another eligible royal walks into the bar." He lowered his lips to my neck, kissing his way up to my cheek.

"I think the ladies will love it. You have no idea how many of them want Sebastian."

He scoffed. "Great. I can see a few fights in our future. I hope your boys are ready for that."

I waved him off. "They'll be fine." We started back toward the bar and stopped about midway there. Low growls could be heard inside. "Uh, maybe you're right. Let's get in there before they tear the bar apart."

Ryker burst out in laughter. "Yes, lets. I'd love to see Lyall get knocked on his ass."

TWENTY-THREE

BAILEY

"Are you sure you don't want me to stay?" Sebastian asked.

Laughing, I pushed him towards Micah's SUV. "No, I don't. Judging by that black eye of yours I'd say you need a break. You're going to start pissing Ryker off if you don't back away soon anyway."

"But that's the fun part." He fake pouted.

I pursed my lips. "Maybe for you, but not for me. I know you just want to keep me safe, but I'm a big girl. One of these days you're going to have your own mate to protect. You need to get used to not being by my side. He tolerates you because he knows I love you."

His jaw tensed. "You're all I've had for the past fifteen years."

Eyes burning, I wrapped my arms around his neck. "I know but now you have your brother. You'll need his help to find our families."

He nodded. "I'll find them."

I wrapped my arm around his and walked him the rest

of the way to Micah's car. "In the meantime, stay safe out there. I'll be here when you get back."

"Try not to miss me too much," he teased.

"Don't worry, I will." I kissed him on the cheek and watched him get into the car. As soon as they drove out of the driveway, Tyla pulled in.

"I see the twins of terror just left," she called as she got out.

I rolled my eyes. "Twins of terror? They aren't even twins."

She shrugged. "They remind me of these twin MMA fighters I watch on TV. They're some sexy beasts. I wish we had wolves in our pack who looked like that."

"We do. We have several who are very good looking."

"You better not let Ryker hear you say that," she said with a wink.

"I don't plan on it. Did you ever talk to Sebastian last night?"

She snorted. "Nah, as soon as he walked through the door with his brother, every single woman in the bar salivated over them. Do all royals have some kind of pheromone that makes people pant after them?"

I laughed. "Not that I know of. I think it's because we're different. The allure will die down once everyone gets used to us. I guess it doesn't help that Sebastian and his brother are easy on the eyes."

She followed me up to the front porch and sat down beside me. "You got that right. Anyway, before you and Ryker walked in on the fight, one of the grays from the Great Plains got mad because the girl he was talking to left him mid-sentence to meet the new royal. He was pissed as hell. The next thing I knew, fists were flying."

"Ryker warned me it would happen. I didn't believe him."

She stared out at the driveway. "How long do you think they'll be gone?"

I shrugged. "Don't know. Hopefully, not long. I'm dying to meet my sister."

"I bet. Do you think you'll remember anything once you see her?"

"She might feel familiar, but other than that, I doubt it. Seraphina made it perfectly clear the only way to get my memories back would be to kill the witch who did it, or make her reverse the spell. The only way to do that is to go back up north, and that's not going to happen."

"I understand. I don't know what I'd do if I couldn't remember my family. I love them way too much."

"I think that's what I miss the most. There's an emptiness inside. When I try to think back, there is just nothing; it's like a blank spot that makes me feel like I'm forgetting something. It'd be nice to remember my parents and to know they loved me. I want to feel it. I don't think I've ever truly felt love, except from Ryker and Sebastian."

Sitting back in her chair, she looked down at her hands, her brows furrowed. "I was in love with a human once. Don't get me wrong, I've been with other men, but he was special. He was so different from everyone else. But humans age so much faster than we do."

"What happened?"

She closed her eyes, her lip trembling. "Once he started to age and I didn't, I had to leave him. It broke my heart to do it, but I didn't have a choice. Years later, when he was diagnosed with stage four cancer, I knew there was nothing I could do. I visited him in the hospital right before he died. He thought I was an angel."

Her story brought tears to my eyes. "I'm sorry, Tyla. I can't imagine being in love with someone and watching them die. Did he ever marry?"

She wiped her eyes and faced me. "No. He died at forty-three. He always said I was the only one for him. On that last day, I told him I wasn't an angel, I was really me. He told me I was beautiful and that he still loved me. I was there when he took his last breath."

"Does anyone else know about this?"

She shook her head. "No, not even my parents. It's frowned upon to fall in love with humans. It's not supposed to be part of our nature."

"You can't help who you fall in love with. I think it's a beautiful story. Not many people get to experience real love. I can assure you you'll have it again."

She sniffled. "You promise?"

I looked into her soft, gray gaze. "I promise. Now let's go into town and go shopping. I have two interviews I need outfits for." We got up and I put my arm around her as we walked to Ryker's Jeep.

"I can deal with that. Anything to get my mind off of love. Speaking of which, are you excited about the full moon next week?" She opened her door and I stood at mine, my heart thundering out of control.

"More like terrified. I don't know what to expect."

"I do. And I know just the thing you need." By the devilish look in her eyes, I was almost scared to ask.

"Do I even want to know?"

She winked. "Don't worry, Ryker will love it."

Sitting on the back deck of the cabin, I propped my feet up on the banister and gazed at the stars, drinking my hot chocolate.

"Did you have fun with Tyla today?" Ryker asked.

I turned to him and set my cup down. "I did. We talked a lot. I think she has a thing for Sebastian."

"Oh hell, who doesn't? How did it go with him when you said goodbye?"

"Fine. I know he wanted to go with his brother, but he wasn't happy about leaving. I guess, until we're mated, I'm still vulnerable."

"But you have me to protect you."

"I know that, but there's a reason female royals have royal-blooded protectors. You have to admit Sebastian has powers that even you don't." A low growl escaped his lips and he tensed. "Ryker, I'm not saying he's physically stronger than you. Besides, you have a couple of powers he doesn't possess."

"Oh yeah, and what are those?"

Smiling, I climbed onto his lap and kissed him. "The power over my heart."

His body relaxed and he kissed me again, his tongue taking claim of my mouth. "And what's the other?"

I shoved my hand between us and rubbed his growing arousal through his jeans. "The other one is so big—so *obvious*—I don't think it bears mentioning." I smirked as I squeezed his length.

Thrusting into my hand, he growled his approval. Standing up with me in his arms, he carried me up to his bedroom and laid me down on the bed. I moved back and he crawled on top of me, lifting my shirt.

His fingers tickled me as he rubbed circles along my stomach. "After we complete our bond during the next full moon, you'll officially be mine. We'll both be alphas of this pack, making all of the decisions together. It's not going to be easy, but you'll always have me by your side. I want you to be happy."

"What about you?" I asked, combing my fingers through his hair as he laid small kisses along my stomach. "What will make *you* happy?"

He looked up and met my stare. "I will be the happiest man alive when you bear our children. We were robbed of our families at such a young age, and to have one of my own is something I've dreamt about for years." Covering me with his body, he wiped away the tear I couldn't stop from rolling down my cheek.

"And I promise to fulfill those dreams. I won't let you down," I whispered softly.

"And neither will I," he murmured. Lifting my shirt over my head, Ryker unclasped my bra. He freed my breasts and suckled them, his teeth growing slightly. I could feel the razor edges grazing my nipples. "I want to taste you. Will you let me?"

I groaned and bit my lip. "As long as I can taste you as well." I was nervous to see what the next vision would be like. Before he could unzip my pants, a howl sounded in the distance. "Is it one of your wolves?" I asked.

Jumping off the bed, Ryker rushed to the window and peered out, eyes glowing. "It's Cedric. Something's wrong. I need to go."

Sliding off the bed, I dropped my jeans and underwear to the floor. "I'll come with you," I offered. Ryker stepped in my way before I could let the magic of the shift take over my body.

"You're not coming, Bailey. I need you to stay here, where you're safe."

"What if you need my help? I can shield your presence."

Growling low, he cupped my face firmly in his hands. "I know, but I can't risk you. Shield yourself and stay here. I'm not going to put you in harm's way again. Just stay close in my mind so I know you're there. If I tell you to run, I want you to listen to me, got it?"

"What?" I gasped frantically. "There's no way in hell I'd ever leave you! Don't ever ask me to do that."

"I just did."

He kissed me long and hard before taking off. I quickly grabbed my shirt and threw it on, racing after him to the door. Before he could shift, I grabbed his arm. All I could do was stare into his bright green eyes.

Sighing, he brushed a finger down my cheek. "Lock the door and shield yourself. If no one can find you, you'll be safe. I love you, angel."

"I love you too."

He kissed me again before the magic shimmered across his body and turned him into a giant, white wolf. His wolf was beautiful and majestic, but also a deadly killing machine. Taking off into the forest, he disappeared from sight.

"Be careful," I said.

"Always."

Closing my eyes, I concentrated on my magic and made sure to shield my presence. When I was in college, I had run into other wolves from time to time, but none of them realized what I was. It was nice to know I could stay hidden. I didn't need them pissing all over my yard, trying to mark their territory.

The phone rang.

"Hello?"

"Bailey, what's going on?" Tyla asked.

"I don't know. Ryker took off a few minutes ago."

"Do you want me to head over there? I don't have a good feeling about this. My father called and said something's going down and to stay out of the woods."

"He's right, stay there," I commanded.

"What if it's the Yukon pack again? You don't need to be alone."

I looked out the window and there was nothing amiss. "I'll be fine. The last thing I want is for you to be here if they are around."

She huffed. "Fine, but if you need me, I'll be there. Maybe Sebastian should've stayed. He'd be there to protect you right now."

"And I'll never hear the end of it when he comes back." I rolled my eyes. "Listen, don't worry. I'll call if I need help."

"Okay, B. I'll have my phone on me at all times." We hung up and all I could do was wait. The wind blew unusually strong, the sound of it screeching against the windows. I could feel eyes watching me, yet there was no one out there.

Ten minutes later, the dreaded news came in from Ryker. *"There's a group of wolves about three miles out. Some of them are from my old pack, and some of them are from yours. They're not moving any closer, which has me concerned. I wish I knew what the fuck they were doing."*

Panic rose in my chest. *"Are you going to attack? Maybe they're testing the waters to see what we do."*

"I don't know, angel. We're all in place, so if they attack we'll be ready. Keep your shield up and I promise I'll come back for you as soon as it's over."

"Please, let me join you, Ryker. They don't want me

dead. I can fight them." My instincts told me to get out of the house and fight. I always listened to my instincts.

"If you come out here, they'll have what they want. Stay there!"

Groaning, I sat down on the couch and gazed out the window at the dark, midnight sky. The moon glowed ominously behind the clouds and it made me shiver. Chill bumps fanned out across my skin and the shivers grew worse. Something wasn't right; I never got cold.

Fear settled in the pit of my stomach and it grew so strong, my lungs constricted. I couldn't breathe and fell to the floor, gasping for air. *"Ryker, I can't breathe."*

"What the fuck? Are you okay?"

"No. There's magic, lots of it. It's suffocating me." My instincts had told me to join Ryker and I didn't listen. I needed to get out to him and fast, but I couldn't breathe. Clawing at my throat didn't help and if I screamed, no one was going to hear me.

"What do you mean? Bailey, tell me what's going on! Is someone there?"

The chills grew worse and I doubled over on the floor and clutched my stomach; it felt as if my insides were trying to rip out of my body. *"I can barely move. All I feel is pain."* Tears fell down my cheeks and I screamed as loud as I could.

"Goddammit, I'm coming to you. Bailey, hold on!"

Fading in and out of consciousness, I heard footsteps on the front porch leading up to the door. I tried to crawl toward it, but I was frozen in pain. *"Thank God you're here. I can't take the pain anymore."*

"I'm not there yet!" Ryker growled in my mind. *"Fuck me. Bailey, hide!"*

The door to the cabin slammed open and all I could see from the floor was a set of boots thundering toward me. I wanted to fight, but I was frozen in rictus. The only sound I could hear was the erratic beating of my heart. Panic exploded in my veins, and when I tried to scream, all that came out was a ragged whimper. It was dark magic constricting me, the same kind that took my memories away. Whoever was in the room bent down and brushed a hand over my cheek.

"Holy fuck. He's here! I'm covered in magic and he's here. Ryker, where are you? I need you!"

Ryker's panic became my own and I whimpered again. I wanted to shift, but couldn't. *"Who's he? So help me God if anyone touches you, I'll fucking kill them."*

"That's just it . . . I thought I'd already killed him."

For a split second, everything went silent, and then every single emotion in Ryker's body exploded into mine. *"How the fuck is that possible?"*

Lifting me in his arms, Kade held me tight to his body, glaring down at me with an evil smirk. "Are you glad to see me?"

My body convulsed in pain. "How?" I choked.

"Now that, little wolf, is a story for another time. I wish we could say goodbye to my brother, but I'm sure I'll be seeing him again soon. It's gonna take forever to get his stench off your body." He leaned down and licked my lips. "But I'm going to have fun doing it."

I was completely helpless and there was nothing I could do about it. His evil laugh was all I heard as he carried me off into the woods and away from my pack . . . away from Ryker.

"Fuck! Bailey, where are you? I can't scent you out."

The darkness slowly crept in, and I could barely hold

on as magic seeped into my veins. *"Kade has me. I can't see anything."*

"Stay with me, Bailey! Whatever happens, I'll find you! Stay strong and fight. I promise you'll never be alone. I love you, angel."

When I was unable to respond and felt our connection disappear, Ryker's agonizing howl could be heard in the distance. I focused on it until I could no longer feel my body. I had a week until the full moon, which meant I had a week to escape.

I'm not weak and I'm not a prisoner . . . I am an alpha. I won't go down without a fight.

TWENTY-FOUR

RYKER

For hours, I searched every goddamned trail. Bailey had been gone for six hours now and it felt like a fucking eternity. I couldn't find her scent, or Kade's; nor could I feel our connection through the bond. She was blocked off from me. When I found Kade, I was going to rip him limb from limb.

"Where do you think they took her?" Cedric asked.

"If I knew I'd be there, wouldn't I?" I growled.

Everyone had gathered outside my house and even though I was outside, I felt like a caged animal, ready to attack. Fisting my hands in my hair, I paced the ground until Seraphina stepped in my path.

"Calm down, son. Being irrational isn't going to get Bailey back. We need to think, to formulate a plan."

"You need to call Sebastian and get him back here," Tyla said. "He'll be able to help."

Clenching my teeth, I huffed and grabbed my phone. She had a point, but the last thing I wanted to hear was him bitch about how I let her be taken. Storming into my house, I slammed the door and dialed his number.

"To what do I owe the pleasure, Mr. Whitemore? Miss me already?" he greeted, answering the phone.

"They have Bailey," was all I could say.

The line went silent but then he came back on, laughing. "You're fucking kidding me, right?"

"No," I growled through clenched teeth. "I need your help, goddammit, so get here now. We're leaving at dawn."

"You're serious aren't you?"

"Just get back here," was all I could say and then hung up the phone. The front door opened and Cedric walked in, followed by Tyla. Clenching my teeth, I looked at them. "Sebastian's on his way."

"Good, but that's not why we're in here. You have visitors," Cedric said.

Huffing, I followed them out the door. Looking up, my yard was filled with wolves from the other packs and the alphas from my council.

Tate approached first, with Kami by his side. "We're here to help. Bailey helped rescue Kami and I want to repay the debt. Let this be the first step in unifying our packs."

"Same here," Ian agreed, standing in front of the Northwestern wolves. "What do you want us to do?" All the alphas in my council pledged their oath to help, including Colton Redding from the red wolf pack and Chase Maheegan from the Timberwolf pack. If it wasn't for Tyla and Kami inviting them to our party, they would've never been so close by.

Standing on my porch, I gazed out at the hundreds of wolves at my command. "I want you to fight for me, for Bailey, and for the wolves in general. The Yukon pack has murdered their way to the top, forcing their claim over lands and other wolves. I say we take it back. They need to be stopped. If you're willing to risk your lives for this cause, then stay with me. We leave at dawn."

With no hesitation, everyone stood their ground. I had my army.

THE SUN HAD JUST STARTED to light up the sky when I heard tires screeching down the gravel road. "He's here," Tyla murmured. I threw my bag in the back of my truck and waited. I could feel his rage.

As soon as Micah pulled in, Sebastian got out and slammed the door. His glare trained solely on me. "How the *fuck* could you let them take her?" He marched over and pushed me hard. "I knew I shouldn't have left." We were nose to nose and I could feel my wolf stirring to get out. Anger boiled in my veins, red being all I could see. Unfortunately, he didn't stop there. "None of this would've happened if I was here. You're the reason she's in this shit in the first place! It's your pack that has her."

Rearing back, I punched him as hard as I could in the face, his blood splattering on the ground. Before I could go at him again, Cedric and Tate pulled me back. Sebastian spit out a mouthful of blood, his wolf eyes blazing.

"I'm nothing like them," I spat.

He started to come after me, but Tyla stood in his way. "*Enough!*"

"Let me go," I growled. Cedric and Tate let me go and backed up. I stood my ground and waited for Sebastian to come after me. His nostrils flared, but he didn't charge through Tyla.

She glared at us both through her wolf eyes. "You can blame each other all you want, but the fact remains, they came and got her with over a hundred wolves in this city. They would've gotten her no matter what. Now shut the fuck up and let's go. We have to work together on this." She threw her bag in the back of my truck and got in, slamming the door in her wake.

I looked at her through the window. "Your father will ream my ass if I let you go," I said to her.

Huffing, she clenched her hands into tight fists. "Too fucking bad. I'm going. Bailey's my friend and I'll be damned if you're going without me."

"Or without me," Seraphina added, appearing from the trees. Dressed in a pair of pants with her hair pulled back, she was ready for battle. I'd never seen her look so angry.

"You've absolutely lost your fucking mind. The pack can't afford to lose you."

She handed Tyla a bag and she threw it into the backseat with a smug look on her face. Seraphina stepped up to me, her gaze sad. "You need me, child. You'll be going up against strong magic. Without me, you won't get far, but with me . . . you have a fighting chance."

"She's right," Sebastian said, sounding defeated.

Micah held up his hands and stepped forward. "What's the plan? We can't all head up there at the same time. The Yukon pack will smell us from miles away."

I nodded. "That's why I have us going in shifts. Some are traveling by car, the others by wolf. I'm sure the Yukons have relocated since I was last there, so I don't know where they will be. That's why I need you and your brother to help cloak me when we're in the city. We'll find out where they're located and go from there. When it's time to attack, I'll alert everyone and have them move in."

"All right, sounds like a plan," Micah agreed. He slapped a hand on Sebastian's shoulder. "You ready?"

Wiping the blood off his mouth, he nodded sharply. "Let's go. We don't want to waste any time. I know firsthand what the Yukons are capable of."

I got in my truck and thoughts of my brother putting his hands on Bailey made me so goddamned pissed I couldn't see straight. It was going to take days to track them down and the thought of what he could do in that time terrified me. Bailey was strong, but she could only do so much against an alpha male and a very powerful witch.

"Bailey, if you can hear me. I'm coming for you."

TWENTY-FIVE

BAILEY

"Rise and shine," a voice whispered in my ear.

I tried to open my eyes, but the sun was too bright. Judging by the smell, we were in a hotel room. The bed was soft, yet every single inch of my body ached.

"Open your eyes, Bailey."

Groaning, my hands were still bound so I couldn't rub my eyes. "Maret," I hissed, knowing it had to be her.

Her laugh made me cringe. "Very good, little one. It's nice to finally meet you."

"Sorry I can't say the same." I opened my eyes and glared at her, struggling against my restraints. *"Ryker! Can you hear me?"*

"You're not going anywhere, Bailey. And don't try to use your link with Ryker, it's not going to work. The spell I have on you mutes your magic. As far as anyone is concerned, you're just an average human girl now. This way, no one can find you."

Clenching my teeth, I tried to break free and couldn't.

"You must not be as strong as you think if you have to keep me tied up."

Smile fading, she glared at me with her two tone eyes; one was green and the other brown. "I've heard about your smart mouth. The only thing that'll get you here is a whole lot of trouble. Is that what you want?"

"I want my memories back, witch. You're the one who took them from me. Give them back and I'll cooperate."

She studied me for a minute and then shook her head. "The memories had to go in order for our plan to work. Why do you want to remember, when it'd only cause you pain?"

"Because they're mine. You had no right to take them," I snapped.

Sighing, she set a duffel bag onto the bed and pulled out a white, silky dress. "That may be the case, but now I need to get you cleaned up and ready to go."

"Why? Where are we?" I glanced over at the nightstand and got my answer when I saw the hotel stationary. Canada.

"You're where you belong, Bailey. In another couple of hours, you'll be with your family."

I scoffed. "Fuck you and the Yukon pack. They're not my family."

"I'd like to see you tell Kade that. I suggest you get used to it because you're going to have a long life with him once you complete the bond. The full moon is only six days away."

"A lot can happen in six days," I growled.

"That it can, but I'm not worried. We're prepared." She grabbed me by the arm and pulled me up. "Enough with the pleasantries. Right now, I have to get you in the shower. Kade will be waiting for you when we get back." She ripped off my clothes before guiding me into the bathroom.

"What's Kade doing now?"

Maret turned on the hot water and waved me in. I stood under it with my hands still bound behind my back. She answered as she washed me. "He's out on a hunt with the pack, celebrating our victory. There'll be a huge feast tonight in your honor. It's my job to make you presentable."

"If I'm the guest of honor, don't you think it'd be rude to keep me tied up?"

Grinning wide, she finished cleaning me up and helped me out. "You won't be bound tonight, my dear. I have other ways to subdue you." Once she got me dressed and curled my hair, she pulled something out of her bag. I couldn't see what it was, but I could feel the power emanating from it. She turned around and held a necklace in the air. "I think this will look lovely with your gorgeous blue eyes."

Pain exploded inside my body and I couldn't move. The only thing I could do was watch her approach me with an evil grin. The second she put it on me the pain stopped, and another bigger problem began. I had no clue what the hell I was going to do.

"How do you feel?" Maret asked.

I glowered at her and at the driver who peered at me through the rearview mirror; he was a wolf as well. "Peachy," I replied sarcastically. I tried to reach for the necklace and couldn't. It was like a force field surrounded it, blocking me.

"I told you I had other ways to make sure you don't escape. At least this way, you don't have your hands bound and you get to wear a pretty necklace."

"What's in it?" I felt weak and nothing at all like myself.

She snorted. "I can't give away all my secrets. Basically, you should feel like a normal human girl. You're not as strong, and you can't shift. All of your wolf attributes are subdued while you wear that necklace."

If I couldn't take off the necklace, I was doomed. Without my strength, I was nothing; I wouldn't be able to escape. Maret glanced out the car window with a triumphant smile on her face. "We're almost home. Take a look."

Reluctantly, I glanced out the window and saw nothing but a vacant road with forests all around. "I see trees," I grumbled.

She laughed. "Exactly. Close your eyes and then open them back up."

I closed them quickly and when I opened them, everything had changed. "Holy shit."

She moved closer to the window. "It's magnificent, isn't it? To the unwelcome eye, we don't exist. It's how we stay hidden when we don't want to be found."

The driver turned down a side street and headed down a gravel road toward some cabins. There were a bunch of them with lots of other buildings. People were milling about. It looked like a small town.

"Did we just disappear behind an invisible wall or something?" I asked.

She nodded. "Only Yukon pack wolves can get through, unless we let someone in, like you. You'll be one of us soon enough though." The driver stopped the car in the middle of the town and got out. He opened the car door and helped Maret out first. She waved at the men standing guard before glancing inside the car. "Come on now. Kade's waiting for you."

Dread settled in the pit of my stomach. Kade would be

seeking vengeance for what I'd done to him. Licking my dry lips, I stepped out of the car, my heart beating achingly hard in my chest. All eyes were on me as I followed Maret to the largest house in town. She opened the door and ushered me inside.

"Welcome home, Bailey. I believe Kade's upstairs. There's also someone else who wants to see you as well. So don't be too long. Dinner will be in an hour."

"You're leaving me here?"

"Why not? You can't escape with that necklace on. And I don't think Kade's going to let you out of his sight. Better get used to it." She walked out of the door and two men stood guard, blocking the way.

Fuck me.

"If only my brother could see you now." Kade laughed. Frozen in place, I didn't even want to look at him. He came up behind me and put his hands on my hips, turning me around. His blond hair was wet and he was naked. I wanted to rip his cock off and shove it down his throat, but I couldn't do that being a weakling.

"He would see me, his mate," I spat.

Chuckling, he grabbed the back of my neck, making me gasp. "Wrong, my dearest bitch, he'd see *my* mate. You're mine now. Once Maret does her magic, you'll be spreading those legs for me anytime I want. I might even have to videotape it and send it to my dear, sweet brother. Wouldn't that be a mind fuck?"

"That's not going to happen. I won't let it," I growled.

Squeezing my neck, he pulled me to him, his arms tight around my waist. "It *will* happen and the best part is, you'll love it." He opened his mouth and sank his teeth into my neck, marking me. I tried to fight him off and all he did was laugh at my futile attempt. When he pulled back, my blood was on his lips and he licked it off. "I haven't forgotten that night you tried to kill me. One way or another, you will pay the price."

Roughly, he let me go and I fell to the floor. I tried to touch my neck, but I couldn't because of the necklace; his bite mark throbbed. He disappeared upstairs and my first thought was to go into the kitchen and grab the largest knife I could find. Before I could get to my feet, a soft hand came down on my shoulder.

"Bailey."

I froze, recognizing the voice. Jerking away, I got to my feet and glared at the woman who had pretended to be my mother for the past fifteen years. Her hair was pulled high in a bundle of curls and she wore one of the dresses I used to love. She looked down at my neck, her gaze sad.

"Don't look at me like that," I snapped.

Pursing her lips, she sidestepped me and grabbed a wet washcloth from the bathroom. "You're going to get blood on your dress." She lifted the cloth to my neck and I smacked her hand away.

"Don't fucking touch me, bitch."

When she lifted it again, I tried to push her away, but she had more strength than me and held both my wrists in her hand. "I'm not your enemy, Bailey. I'm your mother. Now hold still."

"You're not my mother, Annika." She balked at the mention of her name. I couldn't move so I stood there while she cleaned my wound. She smelled the same as before, like lavender; it made my chest ache. "How could you do this to me?" I whispered hoarsely. I refused to cry, but my eyes burned like fire.

"I didn't want to hurt you. Believe it or not, I loved you as if you were one of my own. I still do."

I scoffed. "Even after I killed your mate?" Her eyes went wide. "That's right, mother dearest, it was me. When Darius came and had his men torture an innocent female to get to me, I helped rescue her."

She shook her head. "He would never do that."

"Believe what you want, but he did. Before he could hurt anyone else, I drove a limb through his heart. He deserved much worse after what he did."

Her eyes misted over, but she stood firm, her voice trembling. "I'm sorry I lied to you all your life. I was just doing my duty to the pack." Turning on her heel, she hurried out of the house.

As much as I wanted to deny it, I couldn't. I missed her, and deep down, I still loved her. "Wait," I shouted, chasing after her. Before I could even take a step out of the door, the two guards blocked my path.

"You're not allowed to leave the premises," one of them growled. Over their shoulders, I watched Annika run off into the woods. When she disappeared from sight, I backed into the house and shut the door. I had to see her again.

TWENTY-SIX

BAILEY

I had hoped my mother would be at dinner, but it ended up just being Kade, his Uncle Rollin, and me. "Take a seat," Rollin announced as we walked into the dining room. He held out a chair for me and I sat. What I really wanted to do was shift and rip him apart. It was because of him that my family was dead, not to mention Ryker's.

Kade took the seat across from me, and Rollin took the head of the table. "Are you hungry?" he asked.

I batted my eyelashes and forced a smile. "Not in the least."

His smile faded, his annoyance just under the surface. "Pity. I had hoped to have a civil dinner tonight. Very well, if you don't eat, I'm sure my son will be more than happy to shove it down your throat. Either way, you *will* do as I say."

"Your son?" I glanced back and forth, from Kade to him, and then it all started to make sense. They had some of the same features. *Holy shit.* "So *that's* why you didn't cast Kade out. How is this possible?"

Our food was brought out and he pointed to it. "Eat

first, and then I'll tell you everything." Crossing my arms over my chest, I sat there and glared at him, desperate for the answers. He slammed his fork down and huffed. "If you don't eat, I won't tell you a goddamned thing. You need your energy for the full moon."

Kade smirked and stared at me like a ravenous beast, his gaze raw. Meeting his gaze head on, I took the first bite and then the next. I wasn't going to back down from his stare. The only problem was, he enjoyed the challenge.

"All right, done," I said, finishing my plate. "I need answers. How is Kade your son if you never mated?"

He wiped his mouth with his napkin and sat back in his chair. "As you can see," he pointed to the necklace around my neck, "magic can be a powerful thing. Add its power with the power of the moon and you're talking a magic beyond belief. My brother, Soren, was a good man on all accounts. Little did he know, we fell in love with the same girl. I loathed seeing them together—true mates." He shook his head in disgust. "At least until one day, when Maret offered up a solution. She promised me that I could have a son with Genna, with only one little consequence."

"What was it?"

"He would have to take the form of his brother," Maret announced, walking into the room. I jerked my head in her direction, loathing the smug smile on her too thin face. "In order for Genna to be willing, she had to believe she was with her mate. That's why I had Rollin take the form of Soren. The only stipulation was, it had to be done on a full moon. Those were the only nights he could spend with her."

"She was everything I'd ever dreamed of," he murmured.

I snorted. "And then you had her killed. What kind of love is that?"

He slammed his hand on the table. "I didn't want her dead. She died protecting that son of hers. If it wasn't for him, she'd still be alive."

My blood boiled and I stood, glaring down at him. "A lot of people would still be alive if it wasn't for you."

He smirked and lifted his eyebrows. By the look in his eyes, he had no remorse for all the people he'd killed. He picked up his glass and I smacked it out of his hands, shattering it against the wall. Kade shot up out of his chair and grabbed me around the waist, pulling me back.

"You want to know why you weren't Genna's true mate?" I shouted. Rollin stood and wiped the wine from his face. "Because you're a worthless sack of shit, a cowardly one at that. Our magic doesn't come from being evil, it comes from being good, pure of heart. Your pack is doomed. I hope you all rot in hell."

He stared at me for a bit, before his lips pulled back into a smile. "Son, you sure will have your hands full with this one."

I could feel the rumble in Kade's chest through my back. "I will enjoy taming her. It'll be worth the fight."

Rollin approached me slowly and grazed a finger down my cheek. I jerked away, but Kade held me in place. "Once we build up our pack with royal blood, we'll be unstoppable. I have you to thank for that."

Eyes wide, I froze. "What are you saying?"

He grinned at Kade and then down to me. "I'm saying that when you give me grandkids, our blood will be mixed with yours, turning us into the next royal pack. Everyone will bow down to us."

Chuckling, Kade leaned down and whispered in my

ear. "And I'll get to fuck you anytime I want. Who knows," he said, putting his hands on my stomach, "you might be pregnant with our child by next week."

"*Fuck you,*" I screamed, fighting him as hard as I could. "So help me God, I'd rather die than be your whore." Everything came crashing down on me and I snapped. I tried clawing at my neck to get the necklace off, but nothing worked. Kade attempted to contain me and we fell to the floor. I hit my head, my vision blurring. All I could feel was the pain.

"Do something," Rollin shouted. Maret appeared above Kade, whispering words under her breath.

My body grew heavy and the darkness crept in. Kade lifted me in his arms, and I could still feel Maret's cold hands on my face. "Now she'll sleep. When the full moon rises, she'll wake up and see what her heart desires. You can have her then."

No, you won't.

TWENTY-SEVEN

RYKER

"They're around this area," Sebastian noted, "but I never came up this far north. Do you remember where you lived?" We drove nonstop once we got past the border into Canada on up to the Yukon Territory. The rest of the packs stayed out of range except me, Sebastian, and Micah.

I shrugged. "I have ideas, but it was a long time ago. I remember Whitehorse though. This was our city." For the past couple days, all we'd done was split up and comb the streets to see if we could find any of the Yukon wolves. So far we'd found nothing, not even a trace.

Micah turned the corner, shaking his head when he saw us. "Anything for you guys?"

"Not a fucking thing," I grumbled.

"How is Faith?" Sebastian asked him.

"She's fine. She just wants us to find her sister. The sooner we do, the sooner we can reunite them."

"But for how long? What are your plans once this is over?" I asked.

Sebastian lifted his brows. "Good question."

Smirking, Micah leaned against the building. "I guess we'll just have to relocate. Besides, it's not fun living with a female. It ruins my game."

"So you're moving to Wyoming?" Sebastian asked.

"Looks like it, unless you have any objections."

"Nope, I look forward to pestering your ass. It'll get me off of Ryker's," he said, pointing at me.

I snorted. "Thank fucking God for that." We stood there for a few minutes shooting the shit, and my patience ran thin. Blowing out a frustrated breath, I peered up and down the street. I had to find Bailey. "We have one more day until the full moon and he's already had her for five. Just the thought of Kade breathing around her makes me so goddamned furious."

"I'm in the same boat," Sebastian agreed, his jaw tensing. "We need to figure out where those fuckheads go during the day. Surely, they have jobs somewhere in this city."

As soon as he said it, I had an idea. "When I was younger, there was a man in our pack who owned a bar right outside of town. His name was Abel. I could always smell the liquor on him from a mile away. It was years ago, but it might still be there."

"And you think some of the wolves will be there?" he asked.

"It's worth a shot. Right now, we have nothing."

"All right, let's go," Micah announced. We jumped in my truck and started through town. We passed the ice cream shop my mother always took me to as a boy. Even Bailey went along a few times when she was staying with us. Everywhere I turned, there was a memory. Once off the main road, the bar wasn't far. It was a Saturday night so it didn't surprise me to see the parking lot packed with cars.

Shutting off the truck, I lowered the windows and breathed in. Nothing. "How the hell are there not any of them around? It doesn't make sense."

Sebastian sighed. "Maybe they are, but just cloaked like us. You know what that's like. The Northern pack did the same thing, even though I knew you could sense Bailey. I'm almost positive the Yukons would be protected too. They have Maret alongside them."

He was right. When I left Wyoming to check on Bailey, I knew their homes were surrounded by some kind of magic to keep them concealed. However, I could still feel Bailey's magic through it, calling to me. "Do you think you'd be able to recognize anyone if you saw them?" I asked.

Sitting up in the seat, he focused on the door to the bar. "I'm sure I could."

We all stared at the door, watching people go in and out, mainly humans. Each second that passed, the angrier I became. We had run out of options. After three hours of silence, I started the truck and put it in gear. "This is fucking useless."

Sebastian held up a hand. "Wait." He pointed to the door where two men staggered out and got into their vehicle. "I've seen them before. They're part of your old pack."

I studied them and my memory clicked. "They're Abel's sons, Calum and Devlin. They were my friends growing up. I can't sense them at all." They were cloaked.

Micah scoffed from the backseat. "And there we have our answer. There's no telling how many have been around." Once they got in their car, they drove right past us. Drunk as hell, they almost hit a tree.

"Fucking morons," I mumbled. Putting distance between us, I followed them. Their brake lights came on and then the entire car disappeared behind an invisible wall. "I think we have our location."

"Yeah, and they would get into some serious shit if Kade and his uncle knew they gave it away. When I was with the Northern pack, we had to make sure no one was around before we could enter. Luckily, the Yukons have the village idiots to help us out."

We drove past the entrance and kept going. "How far do you think the wall goes?" I asked.

"Maybe a half mile in all directions. You'll be able to feel it if you get too close," Sebastian replied. I remembered it was like an electric current jolting through your body. I was zapped a few times when I tried to get close to Bailey. "I think we have what we need," he said. "Let's get back to your people so we can come up with a plan of attack."

Turning the truck around, I squeezed the steering wheel so hard, my knuckles turned white. I already had a plan . . . *kill them all.*

"Have you called everyone?" Tyla asked, sitting beside me.

Keeping my gaze on the dwindling fire, I nodded my head. "They should all be here soon."

The sun had already started to come up, which meant our time was running out. The full moon was upon us. Our camp was about fifteen miles south of the Yukon pack, just out of reach of their senses.

Seraphina joined us, along with Sebastian, Micah, and Cedric. "How are we going to get inside the wall?" Cedric asked.

Seraphina answered. "After their explanation of the

shield, I'm pretty sure I can breach it long enough to send a few people through. It's just a cloaking spell, but Maret is stronger than me. I can open it in intervals each time I regain my strength."

I glanced up at her. "Or you can just let two of us in first."

"And who would those two be?" Sebastian asked.

"Me and you."

Tyla punched me in the arm. "What the hell are you thinking? That's suicide and you know it."

Shaking her head, Seraphina spoke up. "Actually, it might be brilliant. None of them will suspect that I'm here to lower the wall, and they certainly aren't expecting Ryker to come in alone. If you can slip in there unnoticed, we might have a better chance. If we go in baring our teeth, Kade will take Bailey and run, or worse, kill her."

"Why don't I go in as well?" Micah suggested. "That way I can take someone in with me undetected. We need to find Maret and kill her. She's the key to bringing down the Yukons."

Everyone seemed to agree and turned to me. "I can't argue with you there, but don't you need to stay alive for Faith? You're her protector. You risk your life going into this fight."

Sebastian nodded. "That's true, brother."

Micah's eyes blazed. "My duty is to the royals and to my family. What kind of brother would I be if I didn't help you? I'm going in there and that's final." Sebastian glared at him, but ultimately gave in. They shook hands and the deal was made. Kade and I had never been like that. We had the same blood flowing through our veins, but he was always different. And now I planned on killing him.

"I want to go in with Micah," Tyla insisted. All eyes

turned her way, but I could see she wasn't going to back down.

Cedric snorted. "Now who's lost their mind? Don't you remember what those fuckers did to Kami? That's what'll happen, or probably worse, if they catch you."

She grabbed my arm and squeezed. "Please, let me go. You need Cedric here to lead the pack when you're in there. I can do this."

Sebastian cleared his throat. "I know I shouldn't open my mouth, but you should let her go." Huffing, I glared at him over my shoulder and he lifted his hands in defeat. "Hey, I'm just saying, it's better than her sneaking off to try and help. I can see it in her eyes. She's just like Bailey."

Her eyes went wide and I knew he was telling the truth. She was going to find a way in no matter what. "Fine, you can go with Micah. Just don't do anything stupid, like getting yourself killed."

She smiled. "I won't. Maimed, maybe. But not killed."

I glared at her attempt at humor and she got serious. "All right, let's get ready to go." Everyone got up and loaded our stuff into the cars, except Cedric who hung back with me.

"Are you sure this is what you want? I can go in and fight," he offered.

I squeezed his shoulder. "You will get your chance, but I need you on the outside first. The other packs respect you and will follow your lead. When you hear my call, that's when I want you to attack. It's time the Yukons pay for what they've done."

TWENTY-EIGHT

BAILEY

"Bailey, wake up," a voice murmured in my ear. Fingers grazed along my skin and I trembled. It felt like an eternity since I'd heard that voice.

"Ryker?"

His warm breath tickled my neck. "Who else? Open your eyes for me, sweetheart."

"I don't want to. It's such a good dream." If I awoke I'd be in a nightmare. I didn't want to leave his arms. "Hold me tighter," I whispered.

He did as I said and I snuggled into him, making him groan as I rubbed my body against his. "I want you so fucking bad," he growled, pushing his arousal into me.

"Then take me."

"Not until you open your eyes. I want you to look at me when I fuck you." I didn't want to open them, but when I did, I gasped and jerked around. Ryker looked at me like I'd lost my mind. "Are you okay?"

"How am I here?" I was back in our bedroom at the ranch. Everything was the same, as if I'd never been gone.

"What do you mean? You never left. You've been

having vivid nightmares, but that's understandable with everything that happened."

I rubbed my eyes and focused on him. It was Ryker, staring at me with those emerald green eyes of his. What the hell was wrong with me? "What happened?" I asked. Everything was a blur.

He sighed. "When Darius came for you and you killed him. You took it really hard. Ever since then, you've been having nightmares and blacking out. It's been horrible to watch you go through it. I've missed you."

My eyes started to burn. I couldn't believe it was all a nightmare and I'd been at home the entire time. Taking his face in my hands, I pulled him to me, kissing him. "Now what were you saying earlier? Something about fucking me, maybe? I think it's time you showed me."

His chest rumbled. "Gladly." Ripping off my shirt and shorts, he spread me wide, raking his lustful gaze over my bare body. His cock twitched and I longed to feel him inside me.

"Please make love to me."

Groaning, his eyes rolled back into his head. "I love hearing you beg. Say it again."

I moaned. "Ryker, please . . ." For a split second he tensed, but then continued his hungry path of kisses up my stomach.

"Are you okay?" I asked.

Grasping my wrists, he held them above my head, tight. "Yep. Just ready to give you what you want." He closed his lips over my breast and his teeth nipped my skin. A growl erupted from his chest and he tightened his grip, sinking his teeth in further. I hissed. The bite was more pain than pleasure. I tried to bite him in return, but my fangs wouldn't extend. When he pulled back, he moaned and circled the tip of his cock at my opening. "You taste so fucking good. I don't think I'll ever get tired of it."

His eyes lifted to mine and I froze; they flashed from green to blue and then back again. Something wasn't right. Before he could thrust inside, I pushed against his chest. "Not yet, baby. I want to taste you first." Grinning wide, he licked his lips and laid down on his back. His eyes flashed back to blue, solidifying my suspicions, and my heart sank.

He stared at me, his body waving with impatience. "Well, what are you waiting on?"

Ryker would never talk to me like that and when he'd taken my blood, I didn't have a vision. There was nothing but silence in my mind. It was as if something inside me clicked and all the magic seemed to fall away, except for the necklace now hanging around my neck. The room I was in disappeared, revealing Kade's darkened bedroom. And when I looked at who I thought was Ryker, was now Kade himself, grinning from ear to ear.

Grabbing the lamp on the bedside table, I slammed it down on his head. It shattered on impact, but it did nothing to deter him. "You son of a bitch," I shouted, jumping off the bed.

Laughing, he dusted off his shoulders and got up. "I have to admit, you're better than I thought. It's a shame I didn't fuck you when I had the chance. I guess that'll just have to wait for tonight. I think I like the screaming and clawing version of Bailey better anyway."

"You do like that, don't you? Why don't you remove this necklace then? I didn't realize you were such a pussy."

His gaze darkened and he slapped me hard across the cheek. My head snapped to the side, tears welling in my eyes. Grabbing my arms, he pushed me into the wall, his body shaking with rage. "You stupid, fucking cunt. The only pussy around here is the one I'm going to fuck until it bleeds. You will obey me, even if I have to break you." He slammed me against the wall again and then stormed out of the room. I was back in the nightmare.

I'D TRIED TO ESCAPE, but I couldn't get out the door without running into an invisible wall. I was trapped. Wrapped in a blanket and huddled in the corner is where Maret found me when she entered the room.

"It's time," she announced happily.

I scoffed. "Time to be raped? You're one sick, twisted bitch."

"Oh, don't look at it like that. Think of it as the beginning of a new era. Kade may have a bit of a temper, but if you give him what he wants, I have no doubt he'll be a suitable mate. Once you hold those sweet, adorable babies in your arms, you won't even care what he's like anymore."

"Do you hear yourself?" I spat, getting to my feet. I marched up to her, my body trembling with the need to shift. "When I get out of here, you're going to be at the top of my kill list."

She giggled. "Many have tried and all have failed. Now stop being silly and let's go. The moon will rise within the hour. It's time to get you ready. The last thing I want to do is force you, since I know you'll be dealing with your fair share of that tonight. You're a lot stronger than I thought though."

"Why, because I could see through the lies?"

She nodded. "No one has done that before." Turning on her heel, she started down the stairs.

"Where are we going?" I didn't want to follow her, but I would rather be anywhere than Kade's bedroom.

The men standing guard at the front door opened it and she stepped out. "My special place. It's where I practice my magic. Your mother is there now, drawing your bath."

"She's not my mother," I snapped.

"No, but she did raise you for the past fifteen years. In my book, that counts as a mother. Now follow me." I walked past the guards and followed Maret, lifting my gaze to the pink sky above. Night was upon us and I could feel the magic of the moon rising. Great Luna, help me. I was running out of time.

TWENTY-NINE

RYKER

"Get ready to go," Seraphina whispered.

I got into place with Sebastian at my side, and Tyla alongside Micah. There was nothing but a wall of trees in front of us, but about a half mile through them was Bailey. I was so close. Cedric stood off to the side and I nodded him over. "As soon as we're through the wall, make sure Seraphina is out of sight while you wait on the others. If we get caught inside, they'll be out here searching. The only job I ask of you at that point is to make sure she gets out. Got it?"

He nodded. "I swear it."

Holding her hands up in the air, the invisible wall shimmered when she touched it. "Maret is a strong one. Lots of dark magic involved here."

"Can you get us through?" I asked.

She sighed, her gaze troubled. "I can, but I don't know if I'll have the strength to get everyone else in. If I can't, you'll be on your own."

I nodded and turned to the others. "I would never ask anything of you. If you want to sit out, I understand."

Sebastian stepped up to the wall. "Well, I sure as hell aren't going to let you go in alone. Someone has to save Bailey."

"And someone has to save you," Micah teased, slapping him on the shoulder.

Smiling, Tyla shook her head and joined us. "And someone has to save you from each other. Might as well be me. I'm in."

Sebastian gazed at her in awe. "Woman, you sure do have a set of balls on you."

She winked. "What can I say? I like to fight."

Taking a deep breath, Seraphina bowed her head, mumbling words under her breath. The wind began to blow and I could feel the magic swirling around us. Her hands shook and her face contorted in pain. "Go now, before it's too late."

An opening appeared beside her and we all rushed in. When we got inside, the opening closed and Seraphina fell to the ground, out of breath. Cedric approached the wall, his eyes wide. "Where did they go?" I stood right in front of him and he didn't see me.

"They're just on the other side," Seraphina replied. She looked in my direction. "Go, my child." Cedric helped her to her feet and she stood in front of me, even though she couldn't see me. "I'm all right. Go."

Now that we were inside the wall, I could feel the wolves. There weren't any where we were, but there were dozens where we needed to go. "Our best chances are to split up. This isn't where I lived when I was part of the pack, so I don't know where exactly to go. Wherever Kade is, I'm sure Bailey will be close by."

Micah nodded. "Tyla and I will circle around and come up from the south side. We'll meet you in the middle."

Sebastian shook his hand and pulled him in for a hug. "Be safe, brother."

Micah slapped him on the back. "Always am. I can't let you get rid of me that fast." He smiled before darting off into the woods.

Tyla waved back at me. "I'll be safe too, Whitemore. Don't worry about me."

They disappeared off into the woods, leaving Sebastian and me alone. "You ready?" I asked.

"Yep, let's go fuck some bitches up."

With it being the night of the full moon, the need to shift would run high. Soon, the Yukons would be heading into the woods to hunt. We needed to get Bailey out before this happened, so when they ventured into the woods, my people would be ready to attack.

Approaching their town square, there was a group of wolves congregated right out in the middle. I studied each and every one of them and recognized a few, but there was one who caught my undivided attention. All I could see was red.

"Whitemore, *stop*," Sebastian hissed, slamming a hand on my shoulder. He pulled me behind the cover of a tree, his eyes blazing. "What the fuck are you doing? I know you want to go after your brother, but you can't right now. Think of Bailey."

"He needs to pay for what he's done," I growled low.

"He will. But this as an advantage. Bailey isn't with him, which means she's somewhere else." We watched him disappear inside a building with a handful of other wolves. Bailey wasn't in there. Her trail was faint, but the closer I got, I could finally sense her.

"Come on. She's not in there."

We circled around the building to a slew of other

houses. Bailey's scent grew stronger the closer we got to the main house, but so did Kade's. My wolf bordered along the surface, desperate for blood. The rage inside me only made him hungrier for vengeance. Breathing hard, I closed my eyes and leaned against a tree to calm myself. Nothing was working. Their scents mingling together was enough to drive me in-fucking-sane.

"Just because you smell them together doesn't mean anything," Sebastian whispered. The look in his eyes said otherwise.

There were two men guarding the front of the house and two in the rear. "I'll take the front, you get the back. We'll meet inside."

Sebastian nodded and took off around the house. The men at the front didn't see me coming and before they could call for help, I snapped both of their necks. Judging by the sound coming from the back, Sebastian had done the same.

The door was unlocked and the second I walked inside, Bailey's scent engulfed me; she was upstairs. Sebastian bolted through the back door and followed me up the stairs. She had to be in the house, but when her scent led me to the back bedroom, I slammed open the door to find nothing but a few drops of her blood on the bed.

Rage overcame my senses. I didn't want to think of anyone hurting her, especially my brother. She had been in that room, prisoner to my brother's sick whims. My own fucking brother.

Sebastian pushed me out of the room. "We need to go. She's not here. Let's keep looking." We did a quick search of the rest of the house and it was clear. Once outside, her trail led us in a couple of different directions. We picked one and went with it. I prayed it was the right one.

There was no one out front guarding the door, but there

were two inside. We slipped in unnoticed. Sebastian took the first one out, while I did the other, his unseeing eyes staring up at the ceiling when I dropped him to the floor.

A voice called out from the other room, sparking my hatred even more. "Roman, what the hell are you doing out there?" It was Rollin. I couldn't even scent him out because I was so focused on Bailey. His footsteps drew near, but before he could reach the door, I kicked it open. It took him a minute to register who I was. And when he did, his eyes went wide in disbelief.

"Surprised to see me, uncle?"

He opened his mouth to speak, but was cut off when Sebastian pulled a knife and sent it flying. It hit home, in the center of his chest, and he fell backward onto his desk. Before he could call for help, I jammed the knife further into his chest, his face contorting in pain.

"That is for my family, you worthless coward. I've waited a long time for this."

Sebastian circled around him and pulled something out of his pocket. "So have I." I couldn't see what he had in his hands, but I could smell it.

My uncle glared at me with disdain. "I didn't want your mother dead. It was you and your father I wanted gone."

Grabbing his neck, I slammed him down on the desk. "Why?" I shouted.

"He loved her," Sebastian answered. "I can see it on his face."

My uncle snarled. "If it wasn't for Soren, she'd have been mine. He took her from me!"

"And *you* took her from me," I growled. Ripping the knife out of his chest, I lifted it high.

"Stop," Sebastian commanded.

Heart thumping, I lowered the knife and glared at him. "What are you doing?"

He stood across from me and showed me the vial he had in his hands. "You're not the only one who's been out for revenge. This fucker killed my family too. He needs to suffer the same way they did."

"What the hell are you talking about? You were part of the Northern pack, Darius' second in command," my uncle sneered.

Sebastian opened the vial. "Wrong, you worthless son of a bitch. I'm Sebastian Lyall, sworn protector of Bailey Storm, and son of Waylon and Milena Lyall of the Royal pack. Your time is over." Rollin tried to fight, but I held him down while Sebastian poured the liquid down his throat and covered his mouth. He tried to scream but he couldn't open his mouth.

"Was that one of the vials Darius had on him?" I asked.

He nodded. "Let's see how your uncle likes being burned from the inside out. It's how he killed your father and my parents." His body began to convulse, blood pouring out of his eyes, ears, and mouth. Pulling his hand away, Sebastian stepped back and we watched my uncle choke on his last breath. "Someone should've killed him a long time ago," Sebastian grumbled.

I looked at my dead uncle one more time before leaving the room. "I agree, but my father loved him. They were brothers." When we got to the door, I took a deep breath and opened it. "I'm not going to make the same mistake."

THIRTY

BAILEY

When I walked into the temple, there were candles all around with a pool of water in the center. Dressed in a white robe, my mother stood off to the side with a sad smile on her face and a washcloth in her hands. There was an opening in the ceiling allowing the moon to shine through.

"I need you to drop the blanket and get in the water," Maret commanded, flourishing her hand toward the shimmering pool.

I peered down at the water. "What's in it?" I could smell various herbs and perfumes wafting off the steam.

Maret put her hands on my shoulders and I jerked away. "It's all natural ingredients from the earth. It'll cleanse you before the bonding and prepare your body for mating. It's also been known to help with bearing a child."

Scowling, I stepped away from the water. "Why don't *you* get in it then? You're the all-powerful witch . . . you should just mate with Kade. That way, you can have witchy wolf breeds running around."

She burst out laughing. "It doesn't work that way, sweetheart. Only wolves can mate with other wolves. Besides, Kade doesn't exactly do it for me. Now get in the water."

Standing my ground, I glared at her and refused to move. I knew the pain was about to come before she even opened her mouth. Bursts of light exploded in my mind and I screamed, falling to the ground. It felt like a thousand knives jabbing me all over my body.

"Maret, stop! Please," Annika begged. After a few more seconds, the pain dispersed and I sucked in a ragged breath. She held me protectively in her arms, shielding me.

Maret pulled her hand back and huffed. "Get her in the pool, Annika. We don't have much time."

She lifted me up and walked with me over to the steaming water. "Please, Bailey. Do as she says. I can't stand seeing you in pain."

"You should've thought about that before you took me from my family." She flinched and then lowered her gaze to my blanket, gently prying the edges out of my hand. Knowing I had no choice, I gave up and let her unwrap me.

"I'm going to give you some time to gather your thoughts. I'll be back in a few minutes," Maret announced. Over my shoulder, I watched her disappear out of the temple. Even with her gone, I could feel her magic oozing all around me.

"Why are you so stubborn?"

"Maybe I get it from my *real* parents," I spat.

Huffing, she finished unwrapping me and threw the blanket on the ground. When she got a good look at my body, her eyes flashed. "What the hell happened?"

I looked down and found a messy bite mark on my breast. "It's the work of your future son-in-law. You must be so proud to know that each and every night, he'll be forcing himself on me. He's already informed me that he likes it when I scream in pain. It should make it fun for me, you know, to be a baby factory for your pack." Walking past her, I stepped into the warm water and sank down into it. Whatever was in it couldn't be any worse than what awaited me once Kade was ready.

Kneeling down beside me, she soaked the washcloth in the water and rubbed it over my skin. "I didn't know it was going to be like that. I thought in time you'd grow to love Kade, just like I did with your father."

My head snapped and I glared at her. "My father was Marrock Storm."

Releasing a heavy sigh, she lowered her gaze. "I'm sorry. Just like I did with Darius."

"This is all bullshit and you know it. I have a true mate. This isn't the way to bring back magic to our packs. By forcing me to do this, it's only going to cause destruction. One way or another, I will get out of here, even if I have to take my own life. I refuse to be a slave."

She finished washing me up and helped me out of the water. I knew without a doubt that whatever happened with Kade, I would rather die than have to bow down to him. The light blue dress my mother helped me in was long and silky, but I didn't see the use in it. It was going to get ripped to shreds once Kade had his way with me.

Through the hole in the ceiling, the moon was almost at its apex. My wolf clawed at me from the inside, desperate to get out. She was trapped just like I was. The weight of the necklace around my neck was a constant reminder of my weakness. With tears in her eyes, Annika brushed my hair and put it up, decorating it with tiny blue flowers that matched my dress. She touched me with tender hands just like she did when I was a child. Even though she deceived me, I had no doubt that she loved me. I could see it in her eyes.

"You're so beautiful," she murmured.

Eyes burning, I grabbed her hands, clasping them with mine. It was the last time I would ever see her. "Whatever happens, I want you to know that I forgive you. You weren't the one who killed my parents, Rollin did. There was never a time I went without because you always made sure I was happy, even when I wanted to go to college."

A small smile splayed across her lips. "You have no idea what it means to me to hear you say that."

"All right, it's time," Maret called.

I glanced one more time at Annika and kissed her on the cheek. She pulled me into her arms and I closed my eyes, breathing in her lavender scent. "Thank you for loving me."

She stepped back, brows furrowed. "Why are you saying this?"

Maret took my arm and ushered me toward the door. "Enough talk, Kade's ready for her."

Giving her one last look over my shoulder, I smiled and let the tears fall freely down my cheeks. "Goodbye, Mother."

Everything moved in slow motion at that point. I couldn't seem to grasp what was happening because everything went too fast. The sound of my mother's growl echoed in my ears just a mere second before I was knocked to the ground. My head hit the side of the stone temple and everything went fuzzy. I could hear the sound of Maret's screams and the ripping of flesh. When I was able to focus, Maret's blood was all over the temple, her body torn to shreds. I gasped when I found not just one, but three wolves standing guard over me.

"Tyla?"

The large, gray wolf stared back at me, baring her teeth in a large grin. The wolf beside her was Micah. If they had gotten inside the wall, then that meant Ryker was there too. My mother shifted and tore the necklace off my body. The second it was gone, not only did my strength return, but my memories came back as well.

I remembered everything about my parents and what happened the night of the attack. My siblings and I were playing Monopoly in my room when my mother burst in and told us to run. Micah had come to get Faith, but Sebastian was with my parents. I didn't know where my brother was, so I had no choice but to go alone. Before I could get out of the house, Maret's magic struck.

I had no clue who I was or what was going on. I just knew I had to run. Then, every single moment with Ryker appeared; from the time he found me in the woods, to the time I had to leave him to go to the Northern pack. We were inseparable and I loved him even then.

"You remember," Ryker murmured in my mind. I could feel him again.

"Where are you? Tyla and Micah are here."

He flashed an image in my mind of a group of wolves closing in on him. *"We ran into some trouble. I promise I'll find you."*

"Bailey, snap out of it. We need to get you out of here. Go with your friends." Annika grabbed my hands and helped me up, pushing me out the door.

"I remember everything."

Tyla and Micah ran out of the temple, growling their impatience. Howls erupted all around us and I knew we didn't have much time. Annika ignored it all and brushed a hand down my cheek. "Cherish those memories, my dear

Bailey. Maybe one day you'll cherish the ones of us. Now go."

Tyla bumped me in the leg and pushed me toward the woods. "What about you?" I called over my shoulder.

She shrugged. "This is my pack. Yours would never accept me."

I shook my head. "That's not true. Come with us. I will accept you. That's all that matters." Holding out my hand, I waited for her to come to me. When she took that first step, I knew I had her. Until, death came up behind her. "*No*," I screamed, taking off toward her.

Kade grabbed her by the neck and slit her throat right to the bone. He dropped her body to the ground and I fell beside her. There was nothing I could do, but watch the life leave her eyes.

"Mom!"

"There's no escaping, Bailey. You're coming with me."

"Fuck you," I spat, getting to my feet. His wolves surrounded us, edging closer by the second.

Grinning wide, he bit his bottom lip. "Don't worry, there will be plenty of that tonight. Say goodbye to your friends." Lifting his hand, he waved toward Tyla and Micah and his wolves charged.

I rushed into the fray, but pain exploded in my right shoulder and I hollered in pain, falling to my knees.

"Why do you have to make things so fucking difficult?" Pulling the blade out of my shoulder, he hauled me over his shoulders and carried me away from the fight. Tyla and Micah were fighting for their lives, as they were strongly outnumbered. Ryker and Sebastian were somewhere else, in the same situation. He was still alive. I could feel his desperation to get to me.

"It's over, Kade. Maret's dead. You have nothing keeping you safe anymore."

"Wrong. You didn't think we depended solely on that bitch did you? We've always been a step ahead of the game. The only thing I have to do is fuck you under the moon and you're mine. Unfortunately, it'll have to be quick tonight. Such a pity. And then once I'm done, we'll be on our way." The fighting grew farther into the distance and everything went quiet. Kade stopped and I focused on our surroundings. "All right, this'll have to do."

He dropped me on the ground and the breath whooshed out of my lungs. I gasped for air and tried to get to my feet, but he came up behind me and pushed me back down, lifting my dress above my waist.

"Now, this is the way to fuck a woman," he growled, nipping the back of my neck.

His weight held me down, my energy depleted after being stabbed. I knew I had to fight, even if I didn't have the strength. "And this is the way to break an arm," I spat. I grabbed his wrist and snapped his arm as hard as I could. He bellowed in pain and I was able to roll out from underneath him, but he came back after me. Turning me around, he held my chin in his grasp, pushing his body into mine.

His arm snapped back into place and he slapped me across the cheek. "Is that all you got?"

"Not even close." I elbowed him in the nose not just once, but three times. His blood splattered all over me, and it gave me a chance to get some distance.

"You stupid, worthless cunt," he shouted, his eyes flashing. Closing my eyes, I took a deep breath and concentrated on my wolf. I willed her to break free, but before I could let her loose, a growl erupted from the woods. Gasping, I opened my eyes to find two steadily approaching white wolves.

"Well, well, look who's here. It's been a long time, brother," Kade taunted.

Ryker stood his ground and shifted, his gaze meeting mine before turning his lethal stare to Kade. "Yes, it has. And tonight will be the last."

Kade scoffed. "You're *challenging* me?"

Ryker narrowed his gaze, his fists clenched at his sides. "I am."

Sebastian growled at something, and everywhere I looked, glowing eyes stared back at us. We were surrounded.

Kade burst out laughing. "Suit yourself, dear brother. I think I'll make you watch when I fuck your woman and then I'll make her watch when I rip off your head. It'll look nice on our mantle."

Ryker's eyes glowed. "What the hell happened to you?"

Kade circled around me like I was his prey. My strength slowly started to return and at any moment I'd be able to shift, but then two snarling wolves appeared at my back. *Fuck.*

"*She* happened, little brother," he said, glancing quickly back at me. "She was supposed to be mine, but you came in and fucked it all up. Even mother took your side when I wanted to claim her."

"And yet you aligned with the man who killed our parents. Your own fucking family," Ryker roared.

"I didn't want mother dead. The plan was to kill you and Soren, and then I'd have her back. But no, she jumped in the way to save you."

Ryker's confusion hit him hard; he didn't know the truth. *"Soren wasn't Kade's father. Your uncle was,"* I explained quickly. His eyes darted to mine and the tension in the air spiked.

"How is that possible?" I showed him what Rollin had done and Ryker's lethal glare turned to his brother. "Finally, I know the truth."

Kade laughed. "I see your mind mojo shit is working again." Then he turned to me. "Thanks for telling him the truth, love. Maybe you should tell him what we did together just this afternoon." Moaning, he licked his lips and faced Ryker. "She sure does taste good."

Ryker trembled with rage. "You worthless, piece of shit. No wonder you're so fucked up. You're just like your father."

"I take that as a compliment, dear brother. I'll be happy to tell him that once this is all over."

"Aww . . . no one told you he's dead?" A fake concerned look splayed across Ryker's face as visions flashed through his mind of what'd happened. He tutted out loud as he shook his head.

"You lie," Kade thundered.

One of his wolves shifted and bowed his head. "It's true, alpha. We found his body on our way out here."

Kade trembled with rage and he started to shift, his voice a deep growl. "This ends now."

"Say goodbye, Kade," Ryker taunted. He looked at me one more time before the shift overtook him and Kade both.

Baring their teeth, they approached each other and stopped in the middle of the field. If Ryker was to win the fight, there was no way we could get out. Not with over a hundred wolves surrounding us. I was about to shift myself when Sebastian came over and growled at the two wolves behind me. They backed up and he shifted.

Flinging my arms around him, I finally let myself break down. "Thank God, you're okay. What are we going to do?"

He squeezed me quickly and let go. "You are going to stay as you are. When this fight is over, all hell's going to break loose. I need you out of here."

"Screw that. I want to fight with you and Ryker."

"No. We didn't come all the way out here to save you, just to have you wind up dead. Don't let this all be in vain."

Tears fell down my cheeks. "What about Tyla and Micah? The last time I saw them . . ."

"They're fine," he promised, nodding at something over my shoulder. "Take a look."

Glancing back, I watched as both of them approached cautiously, passing the other wolves. Once they were past, Tyla ran up to me and nudged me with her nose. I bent down and wrapped my arms around her neck. Sebastian bent down to her level.

"Tyla, whatever happens, make sure to get Bailey out of here. That goes for you too," he said to Micah. "You are the only one who can reunite Bailey with her sister. We can't afford to have anything happen to you." They stared each other down, but then Micah huffed again and stood by my side.

Ryker and Kade still circled each other. They were similar in build, both twice the size of a normal Arctic wolf. Sebastian tensed and looked over at me. "It's time."

Holding my breath, I watched as both wolves attacked, moving around the field like white blurs of lightning. The sound of their feet against the ground rumbled like thunder. They were vicious in their strikes, both snapping at each other and drawing blood. Their white fur coats were stained red. The second I heard Ryker's howl, my heart dropped.

Their blur of movements stopped and all I saw was Kade on Ryker's back with his teeth sunk into Ryker's neck.

"No," I screamed, taking off toward them.

Sebastian chased after me and gripped me around the waist, pulling me back. "There's nothing you can do. It's his fight."

Ryker was on the ground, his body so perfectly still. Kade stood by with his head held high. *"Ryker, get up. You have to get up."* The link to his mind shut down and there was nothing but a blank wall. *"Ryker? Ryker! Goddammit, you can't leave me now!"* The ground trembled under my feet and I gasped.

"Get out of here, Bailey. Now!"

"I can't leave him," I cried, tears falling down my cheeks.

The pain in Sebastian's eyes only made me cry more. "I know, but you have to. Don't let this all be in vain." He pushed me toward Tyla and Micah and they flanked me. "Go!"

When I turned around, I was faced with an army of wolves running at us. There were white, gray, and red wolves, all banded together. It was Ryker's pack and all of his allies. I glanced at Sebastian one more time before he shifted and disappeared into the battle. My heart felt like it had been torn out of my chest. The pain made it almost too much to bear.

"Bailey, we have to go," Tyla urged. I was so wrapped up in my despair, I hadn't even noticed she had shifted. She pulled me in her bare arms and kissed my head. "I'm sorry about Ryker. There will be plenty of time to mourn, but it can't be now. Our pack will need you after this. We need an alpha."

How can I be strong without him? Instead of shifting

back, Tyla grabbed my hand and we ran the rest of the way out of the woods, with Micah guarding us. By the time we reached the edge of the forest, my body was numb. Seraphina was there with Cedric, waiting by Ryker's truck. The second I saw it, my soul ripped apart.

"What happened?" Cedric demanded.

He approached me, but Micah shifted and lifted me in his arms. "Not now. I'm getting the women out of here." Tyla opened the back door and he slid me inside. Seraphina jumped in next and held me while Tyla and Micah took the front.

Cedric passed Micah the keys, his face distraught. "You know where to go. I'm going to join the fight."

Micah nodded and started the truck. "Be safe, my friend."

Cedric rushed off and Micah got us out of there. Seraphina murmured something in my ear and I had no clue what she said. Before I could ask, everything faded away. There was only darkness.

THIRTY-ONE

BAILEY

Light blared through the window, right into my face. When I opened my eyes, I squinted and rolled over. Breathing into the pillow, I laid there as everything came flooding back. The connection with Ryker was gone. I reached out to him, but there was nothing.

"It's about time you woke up," Tyla announced. I sucked back the tears welling in my eyes and glared at her. She picked up a slice of apple and chewed it, not even attempting to close her mouth.

Groaning, I turned over on my back and stared at the ceiling. We were in a cabin, but it wasn't mine and Ryker's. "Maybe it was the incessant smacking of your lips that woke me. How long was I out?"

"Two days."

"Figures." I shot out of bed, straight to the door.

Tyla scrambled to her feet and came after me. "Where are you going?"

"To get answers," I snapped back. I rushed down the stairs and everywhere I went, there were people milling about from the other packs. They stared at me as I thundered past, but my only focus was the people I could see through the window. Bolting out the door, Seraphina jumped and grabbed her chest while Micah averted his gaze.

"You scared me, child. I wasn't expecting you to wake so soon," Seraphina cried.

"Yeah, about that. I'd appreciate it if you don't ever do that shit again. Maret put me under enough." She lowered her head and I instantly felt bad for snapping at her. Micah tensed when I stalked over to him. "What's going on? Where is everyone? Surely, this isn't all that's left," I said, waving at the crowd of people.

"Bailey," a voice shouted. I jerked around and Kami came barreling toward me. She threw her arms around me and wouldn't let go.

"Kami, where's your brother?"

"He should be back soon. A lot of the men went back to gather the fallen and bury them. I heard it was really bad." Letting her go, I turned to Micah and Tyla.

"Where's Sebastian?" We were too far away from the Yukon Territory for me to feel any of our wolves there.

He sighed. "He's alive. There was a lot of work to be done after the fight."

"And I should've been there. I'm going back now." I took off for the woods, but Micah grabbed my arm.

"You're not going anywhere, Bailey."

Growling low, my fangs lengthened and I hissed. "I suggest you tuck tail and run, because I'm not listening to anybody but myself from here on out. I have to be there when they bury Ryker, when they bury my mom. I need to say goodbye."

He immediately let me go, but Tyla and Seraphina

flanked him. "This is exactly why we had to put you under," Tyla exclaimed.

"What are you talking about?"

"We knew you'd be irrational and stubborn. If you'd just calm down and listen, you'll understand why we did it." Her gaze focused on something over my shoulder and that was when I felt them.

"They're back," Kami shouted, taking off toward the woods. I turned around and watched as the men from my pack and the others appeared. Kami found Tate and jumped in his arms while the other alphas started approaching. They were all alive.

"Sebastian's coming," Micah replied. As soon as he said it, I could feel him drawing near. When he came through the trees, he looked tired and worn out. I ran toward him and he opened his arms.

He held me tight and I breathed him in. "Why did you make me stay away? I could've helped," I sobbed into his chest.

"It was a battle out there, Bailey. You're a strong woman and one hell of a fighter, but we all need you alive. We couldn't risk you."

"What good does it do me now? Ryker's gone."

"No, I'm not, angel," his voice whispered in my mind. Gasping, I froze in Sebastian's arms. Was I hallucinating? *"Nah, you're not going crazy. I'll be there soon."*

"Did you hear him?" Sebastian asked.

Taking a step back, I peered up at him, confused. "I don't understand."

He smiled and squeezed my hand. "It's a long story, B. I'll let him explain. But this is why Seraphina put you out of commission for a while. We needed you out of the way."

Taking my face in his hands, he placed a gentle kiss on my forehead. "I'm sorry we hurt you."

For the first time since the fight, I could feel Ryker's presence. Sebastian stepped out of the way and I stared out into the woods. The last of our people came through the trees, yet I couldn't focus on anyone but Ryker. He was so close. I took a step forward and then another, until I was at a full sprint. I couldn't wait any longer. By the time he came into view, my heart felt like it burst out of my chest. His clothes were torn and he was covered in dirt and ash, but it was him.

Closing the distance, he scooped me into his arms. "I'll explain everything. Just don't hate me when I do."

I squeezed him so hard my arms started to shake. "Shh . . . we have the rest of our lives for talking. Right now, I just want you to hold me."

Holding me in his arms, he slowly knelt down on the ground and never once let me go. "I love you, angel."

"I love you more."

"DID HE HURT YOU?" We'd been out in the woods for hours, without saying a word. I had hoped he wouldn't ask that question. "Bailey?" He turned me around in his arms and made me look into his eyes. "Are you going to answer me?"

"It was nothing I couldn't handle. I'm here and I'm alive."

His jaw tensed. "Did he rape you?"

"No."

"But he bit you. Before I killed him, he made sure to let me know in great detail."

Swallowing hard, I averted my gaze. I felt ashamed and dirty for being so weak. "I wanted to fight him, but I couldn't. Maret made sure of that. It was one of the worst feelings, not being able to protect myself. Hopefully, you made him suffer."

He sighed. "I did more than that. It's one of the reasons I shut my mind off from you. I know I hurt you, making you think I was dead, but I would rather you think that for a couple of days than see what I did. I didn't think you were ready for that."

"What did you do? It couldn't be any worse than what I've already seen," I said, furrowing my brows.

"Trust me, it was. The thought that I had to do it to my own brother made it even more difficult. At the beginning, I made him think he had the upper hand by letting him bite me. When I howled, that gave Cedric the cue to attack. When our wolves came through the wall, it gave you the chance to escape. The Yukons were more focused on defending their own lives than trying to keep you captive."

"How many of our people were killed?" I really didn't want to know. The last thing I wanted to do was face the packs when we got back and see the pain in their faces. It would all be there because of me.

He sighed. "We lost eight men in total. One from our pack, the rest from the others." My eyes burned, but I was tired of crying. Ryker lifted my chin and I took a deep breath before looking at him. "They all knew the risks, angel. I didn't force them to be here. With any battle, lives will be taken."

"I know, but I didn't want them to be because of me."

We sat in silence for a few more minutes before he got to his feet and held his hand out. "I think it's time we get back. I'll tell you the rest on the way."

Taking his hand, I didn't let go when he helped me up. Very slowly, we made our way back to the cabins. We were still in Canada and I couldn't wait to get back home. "So what did you do to Kade and his pack?" His body tensed and I could feel his reluctance. He was trying to hide the images from me, but flashes of Kade and blood replayed in his head. "Stop blocking your mind from me. I'm not going to think less of you, or be afraid of you if you tell me. If you could hear what I was thinking a few days ago, you'd be scared of me."

He chuckled. "I'm shaking now." I smacked him on the arm and that seemed to loosen him up. "After you left, all I could think about was you, my family, everything. I wanted to rip Kade apart and be done with it, but I couldn't. I needed him to suffer. I knew he wouldn't bow down to me, so I gave him a choice; submit, or I'd literally rip him apart, limb from limb."

"He wasn't the type to submit," I stated the obvious.

He shook his head. "No, he wasn't and I bet on that. I didn't want him to submit. When he refused, I took out one of his eyes, and then the other when he refused again. It only went downhill from there, as I dismembered him piece by piece. His people watched and some ended up pledging their loyalty to me. Those who didn't were killed on the spot. I wasn't about to show them mercy when none was given to me."

"What about the women and children?" I hadn't seen any while I was there, but I knew there had to be some in their community.

"We let them go, with the understanding they would find new packs and not cause any trouble." We were almost back at the cabin when he stopped and turned me to face him. "I was so angry at my brother for taking you from me.

It was as if I was someone else. I know we're violent creatures, but after what I did to Kade, the thought of you seeing me like that scared even myself. I tore him apart and enjoyed every minute of it. When he roared in agony, I smiled. I took satisfaction in his pain."

He was ashamed and I could see it in his eyes. "If I was there, I would've smiled too. There's nothing wrong with punishing an evil man—brother or not. Kade was soulless. He was filled with greed and a lust for power. Don't ever feel ashamed of doing what you did."

His lips turned up in a small smile. "So you don't hate me for shutting you out?"

Lifting up on my toes, I kissed him gently. "No. You did what you had to do," I murmured against his lips.

"I've missed you too fucking much."

"I can think of something we could do to remedy that, but I don't think we'll have much privacy in the house. There are a ton of wolves everywhere."

He bit my lip and grinned. "Then they'll just have to mind their own business or get out."

THIRTY-TWO

BAILEY

"I see you didn't kill him," Sebastian teased.

Ryker chuckled and loaded up Seraphina and Tyla's bags into the back of Micah's SUV. "No, but I think I made up for it last night."

I winked at him. "That you did."

Tyla shook her head. "Yeah, I'm pretty sure we all got quite the visual with the noises coming out of your room." She laughed. "I'm just glad this clusterfuck is all over." She gave me a hug. "I'll see you when you get back home."

I hugged her tight. "Thank you for everything. You and Micah helped my mother save me."

"She did most of it," she murmured, letting me go.

Micah stepped in front of her and hugged me. "She was a brave woman. Be safe on your way back. As soon as you arrive in Wyoming, I'll leave to get your sister."

"Thanks, Micah. I can't wait to see her again. It's nice to have my memories back."

"I bet it is. Now you remember how annoying my brother can be."

Sebastian smacked him on the head and I burst out laughing. "Nothing's changed in that respect."

Tyla and Micah got in the truck, leaving Sebastian with me and Ryker. "Do you remember the times you asked me to have tea with you?" Sebastian asked.

Visions of those days played through my mind. Ryker tried to hold back his laugh, but he failed miserably. "Nice hair bows, Lyall. I never knew pink was your color."

Sebastian snarled. "Fuck you, Whitemore."

I put my arm around him. "Hey, you're the one who brought it up. I can't help it you fell for my joke. I used to love messing with you."

"And you wonder why I was annoying. It was payback."

"Well played," I laughed.

He winked and headed toward the truck. "It's good to have you back, B."

Seraphina came by next. She kissed Ryker on the cheek and then I hugged her. "I'm sorry for losing my temper. You were just doing what Ryker wanted you to do. I know you're loyal to him."

"I am, but it was also for your benefit as well. You needed the rest and the stress would've worn you down. But I have to say, you snapped out of it a lot earlier than I expected. I'm curious to see what happens when the next full moon rises."

I glanced up at Ryker. "Me too. We've been interrupted the last two times. Hopefully, we'll find out in a couple of weeks." Seraphina got in Micah's car and they headed out. The only people left were Tate's pack. Tate came over and shook Ryker's hand while Kami gave me a hug. "Keep in touch with me, okay? Maybe we can get together with Tyla and have a girl's weekend sometime."

"I'd like that. I'll call you soon." She winked at me and stood by Tate's side.

"I'm in your debt," Ryker told him.

Tate shook his head. "No, there are no debts between us. You helped with Kami, and I helped with Bailey. It's what friends do."

Ryker slapped him on the shoulder. "If you ever need anything, don't hesitate to ask. We'll always come to your aid." Tate and his pack left and now we were truly alone. Ryker had been busy all morning talking to all the pack alphas. It felt good to finally have him all to myself.

"What are we going to do now?" I asked.

He winked. "Go somewhere special. I want to see if you remember it."

We got in his truck and drove to the city. The moment I saw the giant snowman on top of the building, I gasped. "Oh my God, it's Frosty's Creamery."

Chuckling, he pulled us into the parking lot. "That's right. What else do you remember?"

We walked up to the counter and I pointed at the rocky road ice cream. "You always got that. And every time I saw one of the almonds, I'd steal it," I said with a smile.

"Eventually, I just let you have them all."

"You were a smart boy. I had the biggest crush on you."

He brushed a finger down my cheek. "I know. That's why I wanted you to remember. The world didn't decide our fate, we did."

He ordered his rocky road and I got mint chocolate chip, my favorite. It'd been so many years ago and the place still looked the same. We sat down outside at one of the picnic tables and I remembered sitting in that exact same spot. "Your mother used to bring us here. There was one week she did it every day. Kade never wanted to come, he thought getting ice cream was childish."

Ryker growled. "As much as I hate him for what he became, if it wasn't for my uncle, I don't think he'd have turned out the way he did. He had part of my mother in him. It's just the evil side outweighed the good."

"What did your father say when Kade started spending most of his time with Rollin?"

He shrugged. "Nothing really. As much as I hate to say this, my father put all his energy into me. He taught me how to fight, how to be a leader. It makes me sick to know my uncle raped my mother without her knowing it. To know it's possible for witches to do that kind of magic terrifies me."

I grabbed his hand. "Maret tried it on me, but I was able to see through it."

"Were you scared?"

"A little, but not of Kade or Maret. The whole plan from the beginning was for me to have his children and continue the royal blood line. Rollin wanted Kade to be leader of the next royal pack. The thought of being used for my blood scared me, but most of all, I was terrified of not being with you."

Jaw clenching, he closed his eyes and blew out an angry breath before opening them back up. "I don't know what I would've done if I was too late."

"But you weren't," I murmured.

"What if I was?"

Stomach in knots, I swallowed down the last bite of ice cream. "All I can say is, I would rather be dead than be his whore." He nodded, but I could see the turmoil in his eyes. "There's no reason to think about the what ifs. We're here together, that's all that matters."

We finished our ice cream and walked back to the truck.

He was about to open my door, but stopped, his expression guarded. "There's something else I think you need to see. Do you mind making one last stop before we head home?"

"Sure." I didn't ask to where, but stayed silent while he drove us to our destination. It took a while to get there and when we did, he drove us down a desolate gravel road. I recognized it almost instantly. "What are we doing here?" We were back in the Yukon's territory, or what used to be their territory.

He stopped the truck and grabbed my hand. "Don't worry, it's safe. I promise."

Black ash still lingered in the air, smelling of burnt bodies. "Did you burn everyone?"

"No. Seraphina helped conceal the fires so it didn't alert the authorities. We buried the people in our packs." We walked past their village and I couldn't sense any shred of life. It was like a ghost town.

"Where did you bury them?" I followed him to the open field where the battle had taken place. There were mounds of rocks at each gravesite. There were nine of them. "I thought you said eight of our people were killed?"

He led me over to the ninth spot, where the grave was surrounded by flowers. "I thought Annika deserved to be buried with our people. Tyla told me about how she attacked Maret. She saved us all."

Falling to my knees, I bowed my head with tears dripping down my cheeks. "Yes, she did. When I found out what she and Darius did, I thought I would hate her. When she came to see me, I just couldn't. I still loved her and saw her as my mother. Even though I wasn't her real daughter, she'd always been kind and gentle. She had only been doing her duty to the pack. Darius, on the other hand, only loved me because he knew I could bring him power."

Ryker put his arm around me. "I'm sorry you didn't get to say goodbye to her."

"Would you have let her join our pack if she was still alive?"

He tilted my chin up and I looked up at him. "Is that what you would've wanted?" he asked. I nodded. "Then yes. There's nothing I wouldn't do for you."

"Good, because now that we're going down memory lane, there's somewhere *I* want to go before going home."

His brows furrowed. "Where?"

"To the very beginning."

"Do you remember how to get there?" Ryker asked.

I pointed to the next street on the left. "Just like it was yesterday. We're not far."

"What if there's nothing left? By the looks of everything, it doesn't appear anyone's been out this way in a long time." He was right. The trees and bushes were all overgrown, the branches scraping against the sides of the truck.

"You're going to need a new paint job," I said, cringing every time I heard a scrape.

"I'm not worried about it, angel."

The driveway opened up and I was able to see the house up ahead. Closing my eyes, I could picture the way it used to be, all cozy and bright with the aqua shutters. It was my real mother's favorite color. The brick was still standing, but the roof had caved in and the windows blown out from an obvious fire.

"I guess the Yukons set it all ablaze before they left. I wonder if my parents were burned along with it."

Ryker parked the truck. "Most likely, so they could

cover their tracks. Want to go in and take a look around?" I nodded and got out.

The door was cracked so we pushed it open and walked inside. Holding in my gasp, I threw a hand over my mouth as I went from room to room, reliving the night that destroyed my family. "I wish I could've saved them," I cried, whispering the words.

Grasping my hand, Ryker soothingly ran his thumb over my knuckles. "I know, angel."

Our bedrooms were upstairs and that was what I really wanted to see. Glancing up the staircase, I wasn't too sure the stairs would be stable. Remnants of the roof were scattered all over them. "What do you think?"

"It's up to you."

One step at a time, we carefully climbed until we got to the top. Parts of the floor had collapsed, but I was still able to get to my room. Hands trembling, I pushed the door open. The sun shone down through the damaged roof, almost showcasing the total destruction. However, on the floor were the remnants of the board game Faith and I were playing the night of the attack. "It's still here," I said, picking up the dice.

The floor started to shift, so Ryker stayed by the door. "You'll see your family again, angel. Once you have Faith back, we can start searching for Colin."

"True. And at least now he has his memories back." I took one last look around the room, until something out the window caught my eye.

"You about ready to go? I don't think this floor is going to hold up much longer."

Tears filled my eyes. "I just want to see one last thing." We carefully stepped out of the room and down the stairs. I briefly thought about seeing my parents' room, but decided

I would rather remember it the way it was before. Once out of the house, I hurried to the back where a brick wall separated us from where I needed to be.

"What is this?" Ryker asked.

I rushed over to the stone angel statue and slid open the hidden drawer at the base. Inside was a large, golden key. "Have you ever seen the *Secret Garden*?" I asked.

He snorted. "Do I look like the type to watch that shit?"

Rolling my eyes, I picked up the key and slid it into the lock. "It's a good movie. Anyway, it was my mother's favorite. She always wanted a secret garden, so my father had this built." The door opened and inside was the most beautiful sight I had ever seen. The house might've been dead, but the garden wasn't. There were no weeds, and the flowers were manicured as if my mother had just touched them. "How is this possible? There's no way it should look like this after all this time."

A blast of royal energy shot at me from behind as someone spoke. "Unless there was someone around to take care of it."

THIRTY-THREE

BAILEY

Gasping, I turned around and took in the sight before me. "Is it really you?"

He laughed. "It is. I've been waiting on you to come back."

Ryker stood protectively at my side. "Who is he?"

Wide eyed, I stared in awe at the man coming toward us. Everything about him was just as I remembered. But now he was tall, just like our father, with platinum blond hair and strong muscles. His smile, however, was just like our mother's. "It's Colin. He found us." I closed the distance and jumped in his arms. "Where the hell have you been?"

He squeezed me tight and let go. "Not too far from here." Switching his attention to Ryker, he held out his hand. "I'm her brother, Colin Storm. It's nice to meet you."

Ryker shook his hand. "Ryker Whitemore."

"So tell me everything. Where did you go after that attack?" I asked impatiently.

"Zayne and I went to every royal we could find and got

them out before it was too late. We stayed hidden until it was all over. The Yukons wanted you and Faith."

"What about your memories?"

He sighed. "They were gone, but after seeing the attack, I knew I had to do something. Zayne told me what was going on and I put my faith in him. We got our people out and left. We couldn't fight the Yukons and live, there were just too many of them. When my memories came back, that was when I knew you had returned. I didn't know about the battle until I arrived two days ago."

"And you've been visiting here to take care of mother's garden?"

He nodded. "It was the only way I knew to keep the memory of our parents alive. It made me feel close to them. This land is ours. I just didn't want to come back here until I knew it was safe for our people."

"How many did you save?"

"There are ten of us, mainly our childhood friends. Z is with them now, making sure they're safe. We've been training them to fight ever since that night. The kids were sent with me and Zayne to escape, while the adults stayed back to fight. Do you remember your friend, Raelyn?"

I gasped. "She's alive?" Raelyn's parents were best friends with ours. She used to always come over and play with us.

"She is. She'll be happy to know you're safe. I knew you and Sebastian were with the Northern pack, but there was nothing I could do but wait. Do you know where Faith is?"

"She's been with Micah all these years. He found us in Wyoming. Now that everything's over, he's going to bring her to me. Why don't you join us? Bring your pack to Wyoming."

He quickly glanced at Ryker and then back to me. "I don't think two male alphas in one pack will work."

Laughing, my thoughts drifted to Sebastian and Ryker. There was too much testosterone between those two. "Technically, there would be five alphas, but I'm not asking you to be a part of our pack. There are other alphas around with their own territories. We're all united. If you bring in more royals, it'll only make us all stronger."

"She has a point," Ryker agreed.

Colin sighed and then nodded. "All right, we'll come. It might take a few weeks, but we'll be there. I'm sure Zayne will be happy to see his brothers again."

"And they'll be happy to see him." I hugged him for the third time and didn't want to let go.

He tried to pull away and laughed when I held on. "Are you going to let me go?"

"I'm afraid if I do, I'll never see you again."

Chuckling, he squeezed me again. "Just wait until I start jumping out of trees to scare you. You'll change your mind about wanting me around then."

I pushed him away and smacked his arm. "I used to hate it when you'd do that. I'm surprised you didn't do it today."

Ryker snorted. "There would've been a fight on his hands if he did," he stated.

Colin nodded. "Exactly. I'd hate to have to hurt your mate," he said with a wink. Thankfully, Ryker chuckled along with the joke. If it was Sebastian, there would've been a brawl.

"Speaking of mates. Do you have one yet?" I asked.

"Nope."

I winked up at Ryker and then turned back to my brother. "There are a ton of eligible women in our pack. I bet they would *love* to meet you. They swooned over Sebastian and Micah."

A sly smile spread across his face. "I'm sold. Are you two heading back home today?"

I nodded. "I just wanted to see our house first. We have a long drive ahead of us." We walked out of the garden and I locked it up, putting the key back in its hiding spot. "Did you run all this way?" I asked, not seeing another car other than our own.

"Yeah, I keep a change of clothes here for when I work in the garden. If anyone were to pass by, I'd hate for them to see a naked man walking about. We've had a few trespassers come by to check the place out. They think it's haunted."

"Humans?"

He grinned wide. "It's been nice scaring them. They usually only come by on Halloween. The others usually come with me on that night."

"Always the trickster," I laughed. We stared at each other for a few more minutes but then I knew it was time to say goodbye. "I'll see you soon."

Ryker and I got in the truck and slowly pulled out of the overgrown driveway. Colin watched us leave and then shifted into his wolf. For the first time in my life, everything was working out perfectly.

THIRTY-FOUR

BAILEY

THREE WEEKS LATER

"It looks like you have a lot to celebrate tonight," Tyla squealed. It was the night of the full moon and I had just found out I got a teaching position at the local high school.

"Let's just hope there isn't another emergency to distract us this time."

She laughed and grabbed the bags out of the backseat. "Nothing will stop Ryker this time, the man's way too focused. Now let's get you dressed. I want you stunning for tonight."

The sky turned pink and I knew we didn't have much time. Ryker was nowhere to be found so we rushed up to my bedroom and I changed into my brand new dress. It was white, with crystals along the bodice. I wanted it to sparkle in the moonlight.

"You look amazing," she gasped.

We walked down the stairs and with each step, my heart thumped harder and louder. Tyla went to the refrigerator and pulled out a bottle of wine. "Trying to get me drunk on my bonding night?"

She giggled. "No, it's to calm your sporadic nerves. I can hear your heart all the way over here." She handed me the wine and I gulped it down.

"I'm not nervous, well, maybe just a little. I think it's more excitement than anything. I don't know what it's going to be like once we complete the bond."

"I wish I could tell you, but I don't know either. I just know it's the best feeling in the world. Maybe one day, I'll know what it's like too."

"You will," I promised.

The sound of Ryker's truck could be heard coming down the drive and Tyla squealed, grinning from ear to ear. "He's here. Good luck tonight! I'll see you tomorrow and you can tell me all about it." She started for the door and then stopped. "Well, maybe not *everything*. I don't really want to know how you decide to do it."

"Goodbye, Tyla." I laughed, pushing her out the door. She said some words to Ryker when he got out of the truck and he laughed. When he looked at me, he froze, eyes glowing for a split second.

"You look beautiful," he murmured, closing the distance. I thought he'd be in his ranger uniform, but instead, he was dressed in a pair of khaki pants and a white button down.

"You look handsome yourself. I thought you were at work?"

Grinning mischievously, he shook his head. "It's a special night, Bailey. I wanted to make it perfect."

"Oh yeah? How so?"

He held out his hand. "Come and find out."

"Let me put my glass down and get my shoes. I'll be right out."

"You don't need your shoes, angel. We're taking the scenic route." He nodded toward the woods and smiled.

I quickly put my glass in the sink and took a deep breath before walking back outside. Maybe I *was* nervous. I couldn't stop from shivering . . . but in a good way. Taking his hand, we began our trek through the woods, the sky growing darker with each passing minute.

"How far are we going?" I asked.

He pointed to the clearing up ahead. "Just up to the lake."

Once the lake appeared, I stopped to catch my breath. The moon had the most magnificent glow over the water, but that wasn't all. "Ryker, it's amazing."

There was a blanket on the ground with candles all around, and a basket of food. It smelled heavenly. We both sat down and he picked up one of the flameless candles. "Kami got these for me. Using real candles out here wouldn't have been the best decision."

I laughed. "Smart thinking."

"Are you hungry?" He opened the basket and pulled out the food, including a cooler with mint chocolate chip ice cream inside.

"It's scary how well you know me."

"We can hear each other's thoughts, angel. I'm sure there are things you hear in my mind that you wish you couldn't. I'm working on not butting in on your thoughts all the time."

"I have nothing to hide. Besides, if I don't want you to listen, I block you out. Easy enough."

Chuckling, he passed me a plate full with a steak, potatoes, and asparagus. "Same here. You'd be scared to know what I think about every second of every day."

"Enlighten me then."

He pointed down to my food. "Why don't you eat and then I'll tell you all about it." We both ate our plates of food and topped it all off with our favorite ice cream. Once everything was cleared away, we laid down on the blanket and looked up at the moon.

"Why would I be scared to know what you think about?" I whispered the words.

Turning on his side, he lifted up on his elbow and I did the same. He stared at me with those emerald eyes of his and I couldn't help but get lost in the depths of them. "I think about you all the time. No matter what I'm doing or where I'm at, you're always on my mind. I don't know if it borders on the line of obsession, but I can't help it. I love you, Bailey."

"I love you too," I murmured, leaning over him for a kiss. The time had come and I was more ready than ever. Slowly, I unbuttoned his shirt, exposing his smooth, hard chest. "Make love to me, Ryker." I pulled the straps of my dress down and he finished, sliding it the rest of the way.

"You're sure this is what you want? Once we do this, it can't be undone."

Nodding, I helped him out of his shirt and unbuttoned his pants. "I have never been so sure about anything in my entire life." Lowering his pants to the ground, a satisfied growl rumbled in his chest. Keeping his gaze on mine, I watched how they shifted back and forth as he kissed his way up my body. "We're not going to have any surprise visitors tonight are we?"

He flicked his tongue over my clit, making me jerk. My body tingled and I ached to feel more. His warm breath blew across it as he spoke, making the yearning worse. "They know to stay away. I don't want to share this moment with anyone other than you." He licked me again and I grabbed a handful of his hair and squeezed when he plunged his tongue inside.

"That feels so damn good," I moaned.

"And you taste good too," he said.

I was so close to losing control, but he stopped and chuckled as he licked a trail up to my breasts. "I see you want to torture me tonight. What do you think about this?" I reached down between his legs and wrapped my hand around his arousal, stroking his length. He sucked in a breath and pushed himself up and down inside my hand. The tip of his cock grew wet and I wiped it away with my thumb. Licking my lips, I brought it to my mouth and closed my eyes, moaning as I tasted him.

Groaning, he lowered his mouth to my breasts and sucked my nipple. "You'll be the death of me, angel." He grazed my skin with his teeth, but he didn't bite.

"Why won't you bite me?" I asked silently.

Looking into my eyes, he bent down and kissed me. *"I don't want us to be lost in a vision tonight. I need you right here with me."*

I nodded and wrapped my legs around his waist. "I'm not going anywhere."

"Are you ready for me?" he asked, reaching between my legs. Slipping a finger inside, he groaned with how wet I was.

I bit my lip and grinned. "Is that answer enough?"

He spread me wide and aligned himself at my opening. The moon glowed down, its magic swirling like invisible threads all around us. As soon as we completed the bond, those threads would be inside us, tethering us together; Ryker felt it too. Slowly, he pushed, until he was as deep as he could go. I gasped and squeezed my legs tighter around his waist, pushing him deeper. We moved together as one, our bodies and minds fully connected. The bond we already had opened up to a whole new level. Our power merged and whatever magic was in my body transferred to him and his to mine.

My insides tightened and I felt my release coming quick. Fisting his hands in my hair, Ryker grunted with his thrusts, his cock pulsating inside me. I cried out as I finally reached the edge and trembled from the best orgasm of my life. Ryker groaned and pounded his hips into mine as he chased his release, arms clutching me tight.

When he reached completion, I gasped as those magical threads bound us together. His soul was inside me and mine in his, unbreakable. Only death could break us apart. Leaning up on his elbows, Ryker leaned down and kissed me, our bodies still connected. "You're mine now, angel."

I kissed him again. "Always."

EPILOGUE
BAILEY

"Damn, I have to say the full moon really did a number on you two," Sebastian teased. He shut his car door and joined Ryker and I on the front porch. We'd slept in the woods all night and had only been back long enough to have a shower and get dressed.

I got up and hugged him. "It's an amazing feeling."

Chuckling, he let me go and shook Ryker's hand. "And it looks like you now have the power of a royal. I could sense it all the way down the street."

Ryker put his arm around me. "It's strange because I feel like myself, but only not. I can't describe it."

Sebastian nodded. "All I can say is, embrace it. You have an advantage over all the other wolves. Be careful how you use it. Jealousy can be an ugly thing."

Ryker's phone started to ring so he kissed me on the head and disappeared inside, leaving me alone with Sebastian.

"You didn't have to stay until the full moon," I told him.

"Yes, I did. I had to make sure you were safe until then."

"And now you don't have to make sure I'm safe?" I teased.

"Not like before. Ryker can protect you a whole hell of a lot better than I could at this point. You're both stronger than me now that you have combined your magic."

"So what happens now?"

He tapped my chin and smiled. "I'm going to go to California to help Micah and Faith move."

Once we'd gotten home from Canada, Micah had left to stay with my sister until after the full moon. It killed me not to see her, but Micah thought it'd be best to make sure no one attacked. Now our pack was stronger with two royal alphas.

"I wasn't talking about that," I said.

He stared at me for a moment, furrowing his brows. "Are you asking about my duties to you as a protector?"

I nodded. "I just want to know you'll still be here. You're a part of my family."

Chuckling, he put his arm around my shoulders and squeezed. "I'm not going anywhere, B. I like giving Whitemore a hard time, and the area has grown on me. Besides, you may not need me to protect you anymore, but you're my family as well. I love you, kid."

"Kid? You look the same age as me, wise ass."

He pinched my cheek. "Yeah, but I'm almost a hundred years older than you." I smacked his hand away and he rushed off toward his car, laughing. "Tell your brother I said hey when he gets into town. I don't think I'll be back in time to greet him."

"Will do, old man. Be careful and make sure to bring my sister home safely."

"I will. That's a promise." Getting into his car, he drove out of the driveway and I waved.

I couldn't wait to see my sister. Soon, I would have my whole family reunited. Ryker was still on the phone, so I climbed back up on the porch and sat down in my rocking chair. It wouldn't be long before the first snow graced us. I could smell it in the air.

"Fuckhead gone already?" he asked, sitting beside me.

I laughed. "Yes. The sooner he gets Faith, the sooner I can see her."

"You could've had Micah just bring her himself."

"True, but I wanted to make sure she was extra protected. I'm not taking any chances when it comes to her safety. She's unmated and vulnerable."

Holding my hand, he lifted it up to his lips and kissed it. "I understand, angel. I thought maybe we could have a welcoming party for her when she arrives. We could even have one when your brother comes too."

Excitement bubbled in my veins. "That sounds like a great idea. We can invite the other packs. I'm determined to help our wolves find their mates."

"Then it's settled. I'll get Tyla to help us. She loves planning parties." We sat outside on the porch until the sun dipped behind the mountains, casting the sky in sultry pink and orange glows. "What do you want to do tonight?" he asked. I bit my lip and pictured us making love. His eyes flashed and he chuckled. "That's a given, angel."

"I can think of something else," I murmured. It was something I'd wanted to do the night before. By the look in his eyes, he knew what I was going to ask. "Aren't you at all curious to see our future?" I asked.

He sighed. "I am, but sometimes it's better not knowing."

"True, but I don't think I can go forever without tasting your blood. It's intoxicating." Lifting the hem of my sundress, I climbed up onto his lap and straddled his body. I moved my hips against his and took his mouth in a kiss, nipping his bottom lip with my teeth. I moaned the second I tasted his blood. Growling low, he dug his fingers into my hips and pressed me down on his arousal.

"Fuck, woman, you're going to drive me insane."

"Yes, but you like it."

"You have no idea." Eyes flashing, he unzipped his pants and slammed me down on his cock. His mouth widened and then everything disappeared as he sank his teeth into my neck. My mind was like a whirlwind, drifting me from our world to somewhere else. Only this time, Ryker was able to witness the vision right beside me.

"Is this how it is for you when you experience it?" he asked.

I glanced around at our surroundings and there was a magical glow about the place, almost like a mist. "Sort of . . . it always has this magical feel to it, but I usually experience the vision firsthand. Now it feels like we're watching it happen." We were at our house, but there was no one around until a car pulled down the driveway. I looked at Ryker, lifting my brows. "Do you know them?"

He shook his head. The man and woman got out of the car with two small children and they raced to the front door. However, the door opened before they could knock. I gasped when I got a good look at the man and woman. "Holy hell!"

My skin was wrinkled and so was Ryker's. We looked to be around eighty years old in human years. Ryker walked up and stood beside himself, gazing at him in awe. "This is surreal."

The old Ryker scooped the little girl in his arms and she laughed. "Guess what I learned to do today, Great Granddaddy?"

"What?" he asked.

"I learned to swim! I can't wait to tell everyone."

The old Bailey kissed her on the cheek. "And everyone will be so proud of you. Why don't you and your brother go inside and see what I have on the counter?"

"Is it chocolate chip cookies?" she squealed.

The old me winked at her and the kids rushed inside, giggling the entire time. More people showed up and we gazed in awe at what appeared to be our children, all grown up with families of their own. We had two sons and a daughter, all happy with their mates.

The vision started to fade and Ryker grabbed my hand. "Is it over?"

"Yes." I wanted to see more, but I knew one day I would.

Gasping, I awoke in Ryker's arms, still connected. He kissed me hard and held on tight. "We were old," he murmured.

A tear slid down my cheek. "And we were happy."

He wiped away my tear and smiled. "It looks like we're going to be together for a long time."

"I wouldn't want it any other way. You're mine, Ryker Whitemore."

"Always."

THE END

Want more of the Royal Shifters Series? Next up, Tyla Rand has lost her fair share of people she loves. Death is not done with her and now he wants her to pay in Resisting the Moon.

ABOUT THE AUTHOR

New York Times and USA Today bestselling author L. P. Dover is a southern belle living in North Carolina with her husband and two beautiful girls. Everything's sweeter in the South has always been her mantra and she lives by it, whether it's with her writing or in her everyday life. Maybe that's why she's seriously addicted to chocolate.

Dover has written countless novels in several different genres, including a children's book with her daughter. Her favorite to write is romantic suspense, but she's also found a passion in romantic comedy. She loves to make people laugh which is why you'll never see her without a smile on her face.

You can find L.P. Dover at www.lpdover.com
Email: authorlpdover@gmail.com

ALSO BY L.P. DOVER

SECOND CHANCES SERIES

Love's Second Chance

Trusting You

What He Wants

(Trusting You Prequel)

Meant for Me

Fighting for Love

Intercepting Love

Catching Summer

Defending Hayden

Last Chance

Intended for Bristol

ARMED & DANGEROUS SERIES

No Limit

Roped In

High-Sided

CIRCLE OF JUSTICE SERIES

Trigger

Target

Aim

In the Crossfire

ARMED & DANGEROUS / CIRCLE OF JUSTICE CROSSOVER SERIES

Dangerous Game

Dangerous Betrayals

Book 3 - TBD

Book 4 – TBD

GLOVES OFF SERIES

A Fighter's Desire

Part One

A Fighter's Desire

Part Two

Tyler's Undoing

Ryley's Revenge

Winter Kiss: Ryley and Ash

Paxton's Promise

Camden's Redemption

Kyle's Return

SOCIETY X SERIES W/HEIDI MCLAUGHLIN

Dark Room

Viewing Room

Play Room

FOREVER FAE SERIES

Forever Fae

Betrayals of Spring

Summer of Frost

Reign of Ice

ROYAL SHIFTERS SERIES

Turn of the Moon

Resisting the Moon

Rise of the Moon

BREAKAWAY SERIES

Hard Stick

Blocked

Playmaker

Off the Ice

STANDALONE NOVELS

Easy Revenge

Love, Lies & Deception

Going for the Hole

Anonymous

Love, Again

Fairytale Confessions

THE DATING SERIES W/HEIDI MCLAUGHLIN

A Date for Midnight

A Date with an Admirer

A Date for Good Luck

A Date for the Hunt

A Date for the Derby

A Date to Play Fore

A Date with a Foodie

A Date for the Fair

A Date for the Regatta

A Date for the Masquerade

A Date with a Turkey

A Date with an Elf

CHRISTMAS NOVELS

It Must've Been the Mistletoe

Snowflake Lane Inn

Wrapped Up with You – December 2021

MOONLIGHT AND ALEENA SERIES
W/ANNA-GRACE DOVER

Moonlight and Aleena: A Tale of Two Friends

KEEP READING FOR A SNEAK PEEK AT
RESISTING THE MOON

PROLOGUE
Tyla (Thirty Years Ago)

"Are you sure this is what you want?" my mother asked. For the past few months, she had asked me the same question repeatedly. You'd think she'd get the point; my answer wasn't going to change. Looking into her gray gaze, I smiled.

"Yes, it's what I want," I said, ruffling her curly blonde hair. She may have been a hundred years older than me, but we looked about the same age. I was twenty-three years old in human years, but it was nice to know I could live to be five hundred and only have the appearance of a forty-year-old.

I'd gotten my looks and stubbornness from my mother, and my fighting skills from my father. He was thrilled Finn and I were going to lead the pack together, but my mother didn't share in his enthusiasm.

Finn Olcan was our alpha, and currently standing just across the room, watching us. I guess you could say we were having a party for our future union. In one week, we'd be mated and living happily ever after. That was what I kept telling myself as least.

Grasping my elbow, my mom leaned in close, her voice a soft whisper. "He's not your true mate, sweetheart. You need to give it more time."

I sighed in defeat. "That's something I don't have and you know it."

"I know, but this isn't the life I wanted for you. I want you to find your true mate, like your father and I did. You won't ever be fully happy with Finn, nor he with you."

"It's better than being dead," I snapped.

Or worse, it could mean the lives of my family. If Finn and I didn't mate by the next full moon, I'd have a fight on my hands. Not to mention, it'd be a war amongst our kind.

Vincent Connery, alpha of the Sierra Pack, wanted a strong female to be his mate. It was rumored he'd killed his last two after they gave birth to his children. Unfortunately, no one knew the absolute truth. I, for one, didn't want to get close enough to him to find out. What made it even more disgusting was that he had a son the same age as me. Mating with Finn was the only way to keep me safe, as well as making sure our pack was strong.

Finn was a good-looking man and someone I was very much attracted to, but the magic of true mates never came for us. We'd taken each other's blood the night before, hoping we'd be able to hear each other's thoughts. Unfortunately, it never happened; therefore, disappointing us even further. I cared for him deeply, but I didn't know what else to do.

My mother squeezed my arm. "Here he comes, my dear. I'll give you some privacy."

Finn acknowledged my mother with a nod and a smile. "Sophia," he said warmly.

She nodded back. "Finn."

Taking my hand, he led me outside and pressed me against the side of my parents' house, our bodies hidden by a set of bushes. "I love you, Tyla. I know you're not happy about last night, but there's still time. We don't need magic to tell us we're meant to be mated."

"No, but it'd help. I care about you Finn, and I do love you. I just wish it'd happen for us." The only truly mated couples in our pack were my parents, and my aunt and uncle, Sarah and Benjamin. My parents were also the oldest. Everyone looked up to them, yet resented them for being complete. To find your true mate was rare, but we kept praying for a time the magic would come back to us.

Sighing, he leaned down and kissed me, placing his forehead to mine. "Stay with me tonight," he murmured.

I sucked in a nervous breath. "You mean—"

"Yes, baby, all night."

Was I ready for that? We'd messed around for the past couple of years, but we'd always ended it before we got too far. The thought excited and terrified me all at once. I had never slept with a man before.

His hands slid from my neck, down to my breasts; his arousal pressing into my leg. My heart thundered in my chest. He could hear it and a smile splayed across his face.

"Sounds like you're just as excited as I am," he murmured low, kissing his way across my collarbone.

Giving in, I tilted my neck to the side. "Just go slow with me, Finn. That's all I ask."

"Tyla, wake up!" Finn shouted. At first, I thought I was dreaming, but when I opened my eyes, I was naked in his bed, my pulse spiking the moment I spotted him. Ripping the blankets off, he helped me out of bed, pulling me into his arms.

"What's going on?" The look on his face terrified me.

"Vincent's wolves are closing in. They were spotted about fifteen miles out. I need to get you away from here." He grabbed my clothes off the floor. "Put these on."

"I want to stay and fight," I said, tossing the clothes onto the bed.

Eyes glowing, he growled. "If something happens to me, Vincent will lay claim to you. I need you gone. As soon as it's over, I'll come for you." A loud knock sounded on the door downstairs. "Please, Tyla. I need you to do this for me." He kissed me hard and raced out of the room. I threw on my clothes and cringed when I heard my parents' voices down below.

I raced downstairs and my mother's look of disappointment was evident by the scowl on her face. My father and Finn were already outside talking strategies. "We have to go," she demanded. Grabbing my hand, my mother pulled me outside to their waiting car. The guys were standing by the passenger door, and it was filled with luggage and boxes.

"What the hell's going on? Why aren't we shifting?" I asked.

Finn clasped my face in his strong hands. "I had them be prepared, in case something like this happened. I had a feeling Vincent would come for you. He's done the same thing before with another pack."

"And what happened to them?"

He huffed and held me tighter. "He wiped them out. But I'm not going to let that happen here. Now go."

"Oh my God," I gasped.

"Tyla, let's go," my father urged.

Finn kissed me one last time and stepped back when howling echoed through the trees. "Go," he commanded. "I'll be with you soon." He ripped off his clothes and shifted, racing into the trees. The enemy pack drew closer and I could hear their snarls.

"Tyla!" my father shouted.

Turning on my heel, I ran to the car and jumped into the backseat. We took off out of the driveway, tires spinning on the gravel. We were in the middle of nowhere. If we didn't get out of the woods, the wolves would catch us.

"We're never going to get away from them," I shouted.

My father pressed the gas and my body jerked back. "We will. We just need to get to the main road." The night was foggy and dark, leaving everything bathed in an ominous glow from the moonlight.

The hair on the back of my neck stood on end, my pulse racing. Then, I saw a set of glowing eyes in the distance. But they weren't alone. "They're here," I growled.

After that, everything moved in slow motion. More eyes appeared and what sounded like a thunderous gunshot rang out.

"Hold on," my father shouted. He lost control of the car and we went sailing down a ravine. I was jarred forward as we slammed into a tree; the car, nothing but a smoking pile of junk. My father kicked his door open and ripped mine off its hinges so I could get out. He rushed over to the other side of the car to help my mother, who had blood streaming down her face from a gash above her eye.

"Mom, are you okay?" I gasped, running over to her.

She hissed in pain when my father touched the wound. "I'll be fine. We need to shift." Growls erupted all around us; they were close. I could hear fighting from a distance, the smell of blood permeating the air.

"You wanna fight?" I shouted. Ripping off my clothes, I stared the wolves down before shifting. *Come and get me.*

Printed in Great Britain
by Amazon